The Trials of Erin Hays

by Roger Willey

authorHOUSE®

AuthorHouse™
1663 Liberty Drive
Bloomington, IN 47403
www.authorhouse.com
Phone: 1-800-839-8640

Second printing by Author House   09/07/2011

ISBN: 978-1-4634-4433-4 (sc)
ISBN: 978-1-4634-4432-7 (ebk)

Printed in the United States of America

"The only real lawyers are trial lawyers."
Clarence Darrow
1857 - 1938

1

Erin Hays watched seven men and five women file in from the jury room. They had been out less than forty-five minutes. Erin felt sure their short deliberation was a good sign they had decided for her client.

At the next table, Hadley Webb, the defense lawyer for a used car company, nervously tapped his pencil on a legal pad of scribbled notes. His presentation had been a disaster, and twelve people arriving at a unanimous decision in such a short time left the pudgy attorney worried.

A crowded schedule had placed this trial in the only available courtroom. It was large, more suited for newsworthy cases that would attract the press and the curious, rather than this minor civil lawsuit. Eleven rows of wooden spectator benches behind the bar were vacant. Gray limestone walls and high vaulted ceilings amplified even the slightest sound. The room was reminiscent of a somber fourteenth century cathedral.

On the bench, an elderly judge showed no expression as he studied their decision. Then, folding the summation, he handed it back to his clerk and turned to face the jury. Erin felt a stir of excitement as he directed the foreman to stand and read their verdict. This was the conclusion, that decisive moment for every trial.

The judge looked down at two long tables occupied by opposing lawyers and their clients. "The principals will stand to hear the reading."

Everyone rose, their chairs scraping against a hard granite floor reverberated against the bare stone walls.

As the foreman, a burly construction worker began, his deep voice resonated through the chamber. "In case number 946C, Allen Beck vs. Reed Motors, we find for the plaintiff, Mr. Beck."

"Damn it!" bellowed the car company owner slamming his fist on the defendant's table in frustration. The spontaneous movement knocked over a water glass. His lawyer scrambled to keep the spreading liquid from soaking their papers.

Annoyed by the outburst, the judge struck his gavel down with such force it caused members of the jury to flinch in their seats. He glared at the defendant. "That is enough, sir! Any more disturbance from you and there will be a fine added to the judgment!"

The defendant lowered his head, sorry for such an impulsive reaction. He should have settled with young Beck out of court, but his biggest mistake had been trying to save money by hiring his brother-in-law to represent him.

The judge again addressed the foreman. "Is the jury awarding punitive damages?"

"Yes, your honor, we find for the plaintiff an award of twelve hundred dollars."

Erin and her delighted client watched as the judge polled the jury. All twelve jurors confirming agreement, raised their hands.

The judge addressed the court stenographer. "Let the record show that all agree. As stated in the complaint, the plaintiff may return the automobile in question to Reed Motors for a full refund plus the punitive award. In addition, the defendant will also pay plaintiff's attorney fees and all court costs within ten days." He thanked the jury and lowered his gavel one last time. "This court is adjourned!"

It had been a break for nineteen year-old Allen Beck when a family friend and senior partner at Erin's firm assigned two of his lawyers to represent Beck. Associate attorney Erin Hays had taken over the case when the lead attorney, Garrett Barton, became ill.

"You did a great job, Miss Hays. Thanks for getting me off the hook." The lanky young Beck smiled showing his appreciation. "I saved for three years to buy that car and never imagined it would stop running a week after driving it off their lot."

Erin placed a sympathetic hand on her client's shoulder. "It was a pleasure to help you, Allen. Too many of these used car dealers take advantage of people."

They shook hands, she wished him good luck and watched as young Beck hurried from the courtroom, relieved and happy over his successful day in court.

Erin was placing trial folders in her briefcase when defense attorney Hadley Webb strolled over to the plaintiff's table. His appearance was less than professional. Webb's rumpled suit and poorly matched tie displayed an array of aging food stains, in stark contrast to Erin's smartly tailored navy suit and white silk blouse. Two inch heels made her slightly taller as she faced him.

"Well, Miss Hays, it was a turn of bad luck for us when Barton was excused and you took over the case."

Erin knew that his forced grin and lame justification for losing was nothing more than an attempt to cover embarrassment over a poor defense. He had not been at all prepared for trial. His rambling cross-examination of her expert witness, an automotive engineer, had been a disgrace. Webb unwittingly helped her case as he stumbled into testimony confirming the car dealer had tampered with the mileage odometer and falsely represented the general condition of the automobile at the time they sold it to Beck. After the bumbling lawyer had finished with the engineer, Erin felt he had delivered the verdict to Beck.

Her green eyes flashed with contempt as she looked directly at him. "Luck had nothing to do with it, Mr. Webb. You didn't do your homework, and it cost your client the case."

After her degrading comment, he looked down, the forced smile disappearing. Webb mumbled, "Congratulations." He turned, and quickly hurried from the courtroom.

I can't believe that anyone representing himself as a lawyer would come into court so unprepared, Erin thought.

As she finished with the last of the folders, Erin knew her attack on the defense lawyer was simply frustration with her career. During this last year she was finally given a chance to represent the firm at trial. But, on each occasion, she stepped in as a replacement for the originally assigned attorney. The cases had all been minor, on the low-end of the firm's docket. Today was some comfort. It was her third trial and her third win. *I'm batting a thousand; too bad it's in the bush leagues,* she thought. Closing her briefcase, Erin moved into the aisle. Being the last to leave, a now quiet room echoed her departing footsteps.

It was a balmy spring afternoon in late May, 1948, as Erin descended the courthouse steps in downtown Detroit. She decided to take advantage of such pleasant weather and walk the few blocks along Michigan Avenue to her office in Cadillac Square.

* * *

As the elevator doors opened to a reception area on the nineteenth floor of Davis, Clark, Adams & Hays, Erin stepped into the room and moved toward a large circular desk.

An arrangement of bright spring flowers on a low marble table was a colorful contrast to the deep mahogany walls and the massive brown leather furniture. The names of the firm's four senior partners in polished brass letters gleamed against the dark wood. "Hays" was Maxwell Tyler Hays, Erin's uncle. He had been the person instrumental in her joining the firm five years earlier as their only female attorney. She still held that distinction.

"Hi, any messages for me?" Erin asked the youthful receptionist.

"No, Miss Hays. I did give your secretary some mail."

"Thanks," Erin said, quickly passing through heavy double doors leading to the firm's inner offices.

Diane Johnson, the secretary Erin shared with another associate attorney, was not anywhere in sight. Erin entered her office. She dropped the briefcase beside a paper covered desk. A worktable stacked with folders and documents dominated the room. It appeared that more files had accumulated during her absence.

My god, is there no end to it? She wondered.

With a sigh she removed her suit jacket and took refuge in the one item in her small office that confirmed her professional status, a large, comfortable executive chair. Leaning back, she ran both hands through her auburn, shoulder length hair as she stared at the table piled with work. Erin thought about the five years of long hours she had invested in the firm. Her career was not turning out the way she had imagined. When she graduated from law school, Erin had high expectations for trial law, and was thrilled by her chance to join the states largest and most prestigious firm. For some time, however, her dream of a stimulating career had begun to fade.

Although winning in court today had provided some satisfaction, in reality, it had been a simple case and not much of a challenge.

My problem is they like having me right where I am.

It was true. The firm's partners were happy to use her sharp mind for deposition work and her presence in a supporting role during trial, but her involvement ended there. Being a woman with ability had its limits in the firm's male dominated environment.

When the challenge gets tough, you need a man to step in and save the day. Right - when everyone lived in caves! Erin reflected.

Her personal life had not fared any better. Just two months earlier she had ended a three-year relationship with her fiancé after discovering he was having an affair with a longtime female friend of theirs. "Life should not be this difficult," Erin sighed.

Just then, Diane entered, her natural blonde hair in contrast to the drab office. "Welcome back. How did the trial go?"

Erin perked up. "How else? We won!"

"You mean *you* won. I heard about the judge excusing Garrett Barton. The way he drinks, I'm surprised they would even assign him a case," Diane said, lowering herself into the only other chair in the office. The two women had grown close over the last few years, and the secretary enjoyed hearing about Erin's successes.

"What did the jury award?"

"They gave our client his money back on the car and twelve hundred dollars for his trouble. Reed Motors has to pay the court costs and our fee."

"That's great, Erin!" Diane's blue eyes seemed to shine as she offered her enthusiastic support.

"Allen was happy. The kid makes twenty-five dollars a week as a stock clerk. Today he received almost a year's pay. With that windfall he can buy a decent automobile."

Diane smiled her approval. "By the way, I'm sorry I wasn't at my desk when you returned. I was down the hall picking up an interoffice memo from Mr. Davis' office."

"No problem, what's the latest from upstairs?"

Diane was slow to respond. She shifted in her chair. Suddenly, she was sorry for mentioning the release so soon after Erin's return from court.

"They're promoting Goldman and Miller to junior partners."

Erin appeared stunned for a moment as the words penetrated. "They are *what*?"

The secretary was silent.

Erin sat erect behind the desk, her face flushed. "Call Uncle Maxwell's secretary and find out if I can see him today!"

Heading for the telephone on her desk, Diane moved quickly out of Erin's office.

They passed me over again! Erin cringed at the thought.

In a moment, Diane was back. "Margaret said Mr. Hays is in a meeting but will see you at four-thirty."

Erin looked at the clock on her desk; it was quarter to three.

"Thanks, Diane," she said, her voice calm again. "Please close the door. I need to think."

"Would you like me to hold your calls?"

"Yes, thanks."

The devoted secretary quietly slipped out, closing the door.

* * *

At 4:25, deciding not to use the elevator, Erin climbed the stairs. The twentieth floor housed the four senior partners' offices, as well as the firm's boardroom and a VIP dining room.

A smartly groomed secretary greeted Erin with a friendly smile. "Please go right in, Miss Hays. He's waiting for you."

"Thanks, Margaret," Erin answered. Her tone was polite, but her look remained determined.

The senior partner's office would impress even the firm's most important clients. Rich wood paneled walls reached to heavy curved moldings that appeared as if they supported the ornate plaster ceiling. A dark hardwood floor showed beyond the fringes of a deep pile Oriental carpet.

When she entered, her uncle rose from behind an enormous desk. "Erin, my dear, good to see you. Please, sit down and tell me about the trial."

Maxwell Hays presented a striking image, tall, with intelligent green eyes that suggested their mutual heritage. A full head of dark reddish brown hair contained just enough gray to confirm his fifty-three years. He had the stature of a man who would be persuasive to a jury.

"Thanks for seeing me on such short notice. I know you are busy," she said, quickly moving to one of the two large chairs facing his desk. Maxwell lowered himself into the one opposite her.

"Can I have Margaret bring you anything? Some tea or coffee?"

"No, thanks," she answered, sitting stiffly, her hands clasped tightly together in her lap. Erin was sure that Maxwell suspected the reason she had asked to see him was about the two partnership promotions.

"I hear you won the Beck trial. Congratulations! I'm glad you were there to take over for Barton. He's a good man, been with us for years, although I'm concerned about him at times."

"Uncle Max, this is precisely the issue we need to talk about. I've been taking a backseat to the firm's over-the-hill lawyers long enough. I'm sure you know that Barton had to bow out because he was drinking again."

Her uncle nodded.

Erin strained to keep her composure. "In my years with the firm, I've worked as hard as anyone here, put in plenty of sixty-hour weeks. I rarely see Goldman or Miller here on Saturday. Now the firm promotes both of them to junior partners. Miller has been out of law school less than four years!" Her persistent tone was edged with emotion.

Erin knew the position she faced being an associate attorney. Junior partners were the ones assigned the firm's cases. Associates were left in supporting roles.

"I know and understand your frustration," he said, leaning forward, his face reflecting compassion for his niece. "Erin, your work has been exceptional. You are as good at pre-trial work as anyone in our firm."

"That's fine. I appreciate the compliment, but I'm stuck in this limited role with no real opportunity to prove myself as a trial lawyer."

"Remember, you're a woman and one of the younger attorneys in the firm."

"And what is that supposed to mean?" she said, her voice beginning to rise.

"Erin, you know this has been a male-dominated profession since the first lawyer faced the bench. During the war women proved their abilities. The professions are beginning to look at them in a different light, but it's a slow process."

"Fine, so where does that leave me?" she asked, fighting to hold back any sign of angry tears.

"I don't need to tell you how conservative our firm is. The clients want a strong image representing them in court. They pay the bills, and that influences policy. Please know that you are on the promotion list, and your day is coming. Just stay the course, and you will get there. I promise." Erin knew her uncle was being sincere, but it wasn't the answer she wanted.

"I knew this Goldman and Miller announcement would not be welcome news. Therefore, the senior partners want to show their appreciation for your work by raising your salary. Effective this month, the firm is increasing your pay by twelve percent. Believe me, my dear, that set a precedent. Please accept it as a sign the management recognizes your potential."

Erin wondered how much of their appreciation was because of arm twisting by her uncle. She would gladly give up the raise to prove her ability with an important trial.

"Uncle Max, I value your support. I really do." Having him listen was a comfort. Openly expressing her frustration to a senior member of the firm helped, even though they were related.

There was a long moment of silence between them, and she began to wonder if she had crossed the line with her complaining. When she had requested an audience with him, Erin had bypassed her supervisor, the ranking junior partner.

Looking for some sign that she had pushed the issue too far she studied his expression.

Finally, he spoke. "I think it would be a good idea if you took some time off for a while. Perhaps you could visit your mother. I'm sure she would enjoy your company."

Erin did not want to involve her mother in their discussion and changed the subject. "What about all the case files waiting for me to review? My time away could cause trial delays."

He showed no sign of concern. "We'll just give them back to the attorneys involved. Doing their own research will help sharpen their presentations. I'm sure they will appreciate you even more when you return."

For the first time, Erin began to relax. Leaning back in her chair, she considered his suggestion. *Some time away could be a welcome break.*

"Take as long as you like, and see me again when you return," he said. As always, her uncle's counsel seemed prudent.

When Erin returned to her office, she sat quietly and stared at the pile of pending case folders. Erin wondered if she would ever have the opportunity to lead an important trial.

* * *

2

During the week-end, a cold front bringing cool weather had pushed across Lake Michigan. Moisture accompanying the front left shallow puddles of rainwater in low places on the railroad station's platform.

Inside, Martha Hays, still attractive at fifty-four, watched for her daughter's arrival through a waiting room window. Pulling back the sleeve of her sweater, she checked the time: 11:56 a.m.. In the distance, she could hear the faint whistle of a westbound train. The Grand Trunk commuter from Detroit was due at noon.

Right on schedule, the huge locomotive came into view. It roared by, in clouds of smoke and steam as if the engineer had no intention of stopping. Then, the brakes took hold with an ear-piercing squeal, and silver coaches came to rest directly in front of the station. A conductor stooped low from the vestibule steps and placed a small stool on the damp stone surface then stepped down to assist those getting off at Kalamazoo.

Martha moved through the waiting room door as descending passengers fanned out across the platform. She saw her daughter, dodging traces of standing water while moving toward the station.

Erin looked up and called out "Mother!" as she waved with one hand and clutched her purse in the other.

As they met, Martha warmly embraced her. "It's good to see you, sweetheart."

"It's good to see you, too, Mom." Erin answered. Her voice reflected the emotion of their five-month separation.

"Did you check your luggage?"

"Yes, two pieces."

"Let's wait inside where it's warmer," Martha suggested. She held on tightly to her daughter's arm as they walked toward the station.

Seated together on a long wooden bench near the baggage area, Erin felt good about their friendly meeting. After an unpleasant quarrel between them at Christmas, it appeared they both wanted the incident forgotten.

"How long are you planning to stay?" Martha asked.

"A few days here in Kalamazoo, then maybe we might take a trip together and visit Gram and Gramps in Parkston."

"It may not be a good time for me to travel. Let's get your luggage and talk about it later."

Her mother's response puzzled Erin, but she let it pass.

When the overhead door to the baggage section was raised, they stood and moved to the counter. As Erin's Samsonite suitcase and matching cosmetic case arrived, she motioned to a Red Cap. The tall, slim black man quickly loaded her luggage on his handcar. Following the two women he skillfully maneuvered it toward the parking lot. They stopped behind a new Lincoln sedan and Martha unlocked the trunk. He placed Erin's cases inside and closed the lid. The young man gave Erin a broad smile as she handed him a tip saying. "Thank *you*, ma'am." Quickly he was off to help other passengers.

As they drove through town, Erin commented on her mother's new car. "Leather seats and no manual shifting. Some improvement!"

"You know, with the war, we had the other car for eight years. It was starting to need repairs, and I decided to trade it in."

Erin noticed her mother had said "we," as if her father were still alive. She remembered he had purchased the car four years before his death. She wondered what it was like being married to the same person most of one's adult life.

Driving south on Westnedge Avenue, Martha suggested they try a new restaurant on Central Parkway.

"Sounds fine," Erin said. "I had an early start this morning, and now that you mention it, I'm starving."

When Martha pulled into an open spot in the parking lot, it was almost one o'clock, and people were beginning to leave. As soon as they entered, a pleasant young hostess led them to a booth by a window overlooking the parkway and left two menus.

After they ordered, Martha asked, "Well, how have you been, dear?" She was careful to keep the question vague to avoid raising the issue of Erin's struggle with her career, a topic that had caused friction between them this past year.

"They gave me a generous pay increase. I guess it's supposed to keep me satisfied doing research work while they promote male attorneys around me. There was an announcement of two new junior partners again this past week."

"What does Maxwell have to say about your position with the firm?"

"He tells me to be patient. He does what he can, but Frank Davis, the managing partner, has the final say on promotions and policy. There is only so much Uncle Max can do. I'm sure he was the one behind my raise."

Erin looked away from her mother and stared out the parkway window. Talking about her situation at work renewed Erin's frustration. "Sorry, Mom. Sometimes it just gets the best of me."

Martha was silent, thinking for the hundredth time that Erin's ambition to be a trial lawyer was going against a natural order in life and was the source of her daughter's problems. To Erin's mother, having an education was fine, but it was a man's place to brave the world for a living. She struggled with the notion that her beautiful daughter, who had always attracted so many young men, was nearly thirty and still single. Martha's thoughts faded as a waitress appeared, balancing their food on a tray high above her head.

While they ate, Erin again mentioned visiting her grandparents' farm.

"Let's just enjoy lunch and talk about it when we get back to the house," Martha answered, once more putting off the subject.

Erin shrugged and decided not to press the issue, but she had a strong feeling she would be making the trip alone.

When lunch was over and the check arrived, Erin quickly picked it up. "My treat; I might as well start spending some of that raise," she said with a sigh.

"Thank you, sweetheart," Martha responded. "Since you are buying lunch, I'll provide the ride home."

"Gee, thanks, Mom!" Erin said smiling for the first time. She appreciated her mother's effort to lighten the moment.

Erin was paying the cashier when a deep male voice called out her name, "Erin Hays, is that you?"

She turned and saw a tall, muscular man in a tweed sport jacket and recognized him as Tom Jackson, her old boyfriend. A wide smile showed under a carefully trimmed mustache that matched the color of his blond, neatly-combed hair. He looked even more handsome than she remembered.

"Hello, Tom!"

"Are you back in town to stay?" he asked.

"Just here for a few days visiting Mom. Working at a law firm in Detroit."

"You look great, Erin! You're still the best looking woman in town," he said, gazing into the green eyes that had always fascinated him.

"And you're still the same old Tom, smooth as ever."

"No kidding, Erin, it's great to see you again!" His tone sounded sincere, and he appeared more mature. She hadn't seen him since leaving Kalamazoo to enter law school in Ann Arbor.

"I don't see a ring on your finger," he commented.

"No, I'm still single."

Tom noticed Erin's mother standing near the entrance and waved. Martha smiled and waved back, then stepped through the restaurant door.

Erin looked into the handsome face and clear blue eyes that had once attracted her into foolish daydreaming.

"Mom is leaving. It was good to see you again, Tom." She flashed a quick smile then turned to go.

Outside, Erin caught up to her mother by the car. "Wasn't that Tom Jackson?" Martha asked across the car roof while opening the driver's side door.

"It certainly was," Erin responded, as she slid into the front seat next to her mother.

"Such a *nice* young man and handsome, too," Martha said starting the car.

Erin wondered what her mother would think if she knew that Tom Jackson had taken her daughter's virginity on their living room couch one night the year before she left to enter law school at Ann Arbor.

* * *

The big sedan eased up a long hill on Oakland Drive, past sprawling lawns of the State Hospital. In just over a mile, they turned down Franklin Lane to a large colonial style house that had been home to Erin from the time she was eight years old.

When Erin saw the shady yard with freshly mowed grass, it brought back old memories of running through a sprinkler with neighborhood friends on hot summer days.

"Well, here we are," Martha said as she stopped the car in the driveway at a side entrance. "If we park here, it will be easier to bring your luggage inside. I can put the car in the garage later."

Upstairs in her bedroom, Erin sat quietly for a time in the special white rocking chair that had been a tenth birthday present. Everything around her was just the same as when she had left for law school. Her mother had redecorated the entire house except for Erin's room. The same pictures and school pennants hung on the walls; her high school tennis trophies were still in their original places. It was as if she had never left. She noticed photos of past friends were beginning to look a little dated.

As she rocked, Erin stared at her mother's wedding picture on the dresser. She recalled the story of how her father had been so impressed when introduced to the beautiful young woman from Iowa that he had called her for a date. They were married the following year.

Erin was happy with her comfortable townhouse on Riverside Drive in Detroit, but it was good to be home again.

* * *

Some time later, Erin found her mother seated in a cozy porch overlooking the backyard. It was mid-afternoon, and the sun was beginning to peek through parting clouds. Outside, birds chattered to prospective mates as they flew back and forth among new leaves in the tall maple trees.

Erin lowered herself into a cushioned chair facing her mother. A fresh pitcher of iced tea sat on a wrought-iron cocktail table.

"Upstairs in my old room, I was thinking how good it feels to be home again," Erin said, pouring herself a glass.

"Why not spend your time here?" her mother offered. "You can visit with friends and do as you please for a while."

"I need to get away. Being here feels too close to Detroit and the firm. I thought the farm would be a good place to think about my future while just relaxing in the quiet country."

Erin's mother was silent. She looked away then back to her daughter. "I have been seeing Paul Morrison."

"Yes, I know that you were."

"I told him you would be coming today and suggested the three of us might have dinner tomorrow night at the club. Is that all right?"

"Yes. I always liked Doctor Paul. It was too bad when he lost his wife. I think it's good the two of you can spend time together."

Martha paused as if not sure of what to say next. Then she spoke. "We wanted you to be the first to know that Paul has asked me to marry him, and I have accepted."

For a moment Erin was silent.

"Well, don't just stare at me. Say something!"

"You're getting married?"

"Yes, to Paul Morrison!"

At the news, Erin quickly moved from the chair and hugged her mother.

"I think it's wonderful Mom! You need to have someone in your life. You have been alone in this big house too long." Now it was clear to Erin why her mother had put off discussing the trip. She had a new life to think about.

"Where will the two of you live?" Erin asked, back in her chair again.

"We talked about living either here or in his home. Finally, we decided it would be best to start fresh in our own place. Paul owns a large, wooded lot, and we have started to build. It's a dream I've had for a long time. When your father died, I never thought it would happen, but now it has."

"What about your marriage plans?" Erin asked blowing her nose on a tissue.

"I told Paul we should wait until October. That's when our contractor promised to have our house completed."

* * *

The next evening, Erin and her mother had dinner with "Dr. Paul."

15

Erin enjoyed seeing the couple happy and excited with all their plans. Yet, deep inside there was the feeling that she should be the one looking forward to her own wedding.

During the night, Erin dreamed she was dressed in a beautiful gown. She walked down a church aisle on her father's arm. Her mother, Uncle Maxwell, his wife, Betty, and Diane Johnson were in the first row, beaming as she approached. Erin stopped when she saw it was Tom Jackson waiting for her in his tweed sport jacket, blond hair and wide, toothy smile. At the podium, dressed in a black suit and turned collar, was Dr Paul Morrison. He was holding a Bible.

"Wait, Daddy! I can't marry Tom! I don't love him!" Then she started to cry as her father took her in his arms.

"Now, now, dear," he said, "everything is fine. Your mother and I love you, and she likes Tom. He's such a nice young man."

Then everything faded away with Erin still crying that she wouldn't marry Tom.

* * *

In the morning Erin woke, vaguely remembering the dream. She stretched with a noisy yawn and ran her fingers through her ruffled hair.

"Boy, that was weird!" she said aloud. She jumped out of bed, pulled off her pajamas, and grabbed her old terry robe. Still amused at her crazy dream, she hurried to the hall bathroom and into the shower.

As spray splashed over her body, she remembered when her mother would call upstairs with orders not to use up all their hot water. Even on this first morning away from work, frustrations over her career were beginning to feel distant.

Afterward, rummaging through the bedroom closet, she found a faded sweatshirt, jeans and tennis shoes. She wondered if they would still fit.

When she breezed into the kitchen, her mother had juice, toast and coffee waiting. "Good morning. You're dressed as if heading back to high school," her mother said, sounding surprised.

Erin took her original place at the table. "Just trying on some of my old clothes to see if I could still get into them."

She noticed the serious look on her mother's face. "What's on your mind, Mom?"

"I hope you're not upset about my selling the house?"

"What made you think that I would be upset?"

"Well, I wasn't sure how you would feel about the marriage, and I was afraid that selling the home where you grew up might be a problem for you."

"Why?"

"I thought you might feel disappointed that I had made that decision before telling you."

"Hey, Mom, I told you last night it's great that you're getting married again. I'm excited for you and look forward to seeing your new home."

Erin could see relief in her mother's expression.

"Well, I'm glad. There is so much to think about, and I've been feeling guilty for comments I made to you at Christmas about your career and breaking off your engagement. It's just not the right time for me to leave on a trip."

"Mother, I understand. It will be good to see Gram and Gramps again, but you know how low-key it is at their farm. I will probably be so bored in a week that I'll be on the train heading back to Michigan."

* * *

Later that day, Erin and her mother drove to the site where the new house was under construction. It was a pleasant setting with mature trees on a spacious lot that rose gently from the street. She was glad that her mother's dream would be coming true.

When they returned home, Tom Jackson surprised Erin when he called suggesting they have lunch the following day. With nothing better to do, she reluctantly agreed.

When Erin returned home that afternoon, her mother asked if she had enjoyed her time with Tom.

"Well, if you like being with someone who spends the entire meal complaining about his ex-wife and bragging about what a great supervisor he is at the paper mill, then Tom's your man. The high point was his suggestion that we should think about seeing each other again now that his divorce is final. Don't say it, Mom! Tom seems like such a *nice* young man, and I'm too picky!"

That evening, Erin and her mother ate dinner at home. Later, they sat on the back porch talking until bedtime. The following afternoon, Martha drove her daughter to the station.

* * *

3

The sky was overcast as Martha dropped Erin at the train station door. After finding a place to park, she joined her daughter inside near the baggage area.

Erin glanced at the bright red letters on her suitcase claim check, spelling out tomorrow's destination, Cherokee. It was Illinois Central's nearest passenger stop to Taylor's farm and the small town of Parkston, Iowa.

"Are you all set?" Martha asked.

"Yes, they have my case and I'm ready."

Martha mentioned the balmy weather and they decided to wait outside. Hanging on to her purse, Erin lifted the cosmetic bag that she would need on her overnight sleeper out of Chicago as the two women headed for the station platform.

"Take care of yourself and call me when you get there," Martha said as they stood together watching for the train.

"Don't worry, Mother. Everything will be just fine. Gram said she and Gramps will meet me in Cherokee. When we arrive at the farm, I'll give you a call."

"I know you'll be fine traveling alone. I'm just feeling I should be going with you."

"Please, you have a busy schedule with the new house and a wedding to plan. I'll be soaking up all that fresh country air and just taking it easy."

At the sound of a train approaching, Martha gave her daughter's arm a firm squeeze. In a moment, the massive engine of the Grand

Trunk's Twilight Limited roared noisily by with such force that it made the stone platform vibrate beneath their feet. The coaches came to a slow, screeching stop.

Erin tried to avoid watching the tears welling in her mother's eyes now that it was time to say good-bye. After a final hug, Erin broke from their embrace and climbed the steps onto her waiting train.

Once on board, Erin moved down the aisle to look for a seat where she could view the station. Still waiting on the platform, Martha saw her daughter through the window and waved. As the train started to edge away, Erin waved back until her mother disappeared from view. Releasing the emotion of their parting she let out a sigh.

The coach was only partially filled and the seat next to Erin was empty providing plenty of space to stretch out. Large side windows and high ceilings gave the coach a roomy feeling, and Erin pulled a lever to recline her seatback. It would be three hours before the Limited was due in Chicago.

Lost in the motion of the speeding train, she half dozed, thinking of her mother about to start a new life in a second marriage. *Why was it so hard for me to find someone?* She had thought her fiancé, Terry Warner, would be that person, but he had turned out to be a sad disappointment. Maybe she should have given their relationship another chance. Maybe at her grandparents' farm she would find some answers.

* * *

4

The Twilight Limited completed its one hundred and fifty seven mile trip to Chicago. It arrived on time.

In the lower track area of the massive Illinois Central Station, Erin stepped down from her day coach and moved along a concrete walkway that separated rows of waiting trains. As she passed, bursts of steam hissed, and condensed water dripped onto the tracks like hot breath from tired beasts at the end of a labored journey. The air was warm and muggy.

At the end of the walkway, Erin, along with other passengers, moved quickly up a wide stairway leading to the main level. As she entered IC's huge concourse, the air was cool again, and she felt a sense of excitement being in such an immense place. The towering ceiling looked down on a sea of hardwood benches. The massive room's stark surfaces reflected the sounds of travelers' movements in overlapping echoes.

A huge clock on the far wall showed it was 5:58 in the evening. Her wristwatch showed it was almost seven. Then she remembered that Chicago was in the Central Time Zone. She adjusted her watch back one hour

Erin wondered if her departing train was ready for boarding.

On a nearby bench, a stocky man in a conductor's uniform had his face buried in the *Chicago Tribune's* sports section.

Erin approached, politely asking, "Excuse me, sir, can you help me?"

He looked up. "What is it?" he asked.

"The schedule shows my train leaving at seven. I wonder if it would be ready to board this soon?"

"May I see your ticket?" She handed it to him and waited. He studied it for a moment then glanced at a large train board located above the passenger gates.

"That would be the Hawkeye, train number eleven on track fifteen. It's a sleeper; you can board it up to one hour before departure. I see it is nearly six, so it should be ready now. Take portal "C." It will lead you down to your train."

Erin smiled and thanked him. Turning away, she noticed a newsstand across the terminal area and decided to buy a magazine. While waiting in line to pay for a *Reader's Digest*, she overheard the man in front of her speak with a heavy accent to the clerk as he bought two Cuban cigars. He wore a dark blue suit and was large and muscular. Moving to leave, he bumped Erin's arm with such force that it knocked the magazine out of her hand. Startled, she looked up catching a glimpse of his face. There was a hard, almost sinister look about him. A light scar on his left cheek just below his eye added to his menacing appearance. He continued walking, ignoring the incident as if it had never happened.

"Thanks a lot, mister!" Erin said loud enough that he could have heard her comment. The big man continued to walk away. "What a jerk!" she muttered while bending down to recover the magazine. Erin hoped he hadn't heard her last comment, as she didn't want to confront him.

"I wouldn't want to meet that guy in a dark alley," said the wide-eyed woman behind the counter.

"Neither would I!" responded Erin, shaking her head as she paid for the magazine.

The event soon faded from her thoughts as she concentrated on heading for portal "C" and westbound departures.

At the bottom of the steps where the concrete walkways began, Erin saw a sign: "Hawkeye No. 11" next to a train backed into the boarding area. On the sides of the dark brown coaches were the words: "PULLMAN SLEEPING CAR" in large gold letters.

A conductor stood next to a low stool by the second coach. As she approached, he greeted Erin and asked to check her ticket. "I see you're going all the way to Cherokee. Your car is to the left." He took her arm and guided her up the first step. "The porter will help you find your berth. Enjoy your trip."

As the sleeping car's door closed, silence surrounded her like a soft blanket, leaving behind noise from the vast staging area outside. Holding tightly to her purse and overnight case, Erin moved down the narrow hallway past a women's lounge and the car's only private compartment. From that point, the hall made a right turn, opening into an aisle that separated long rows of heavy, dark green curtains.

She saw the porter making up the last berth. He noticed Erin coming toward him and quickly moved to greet her. "Good evening, ma'am, welcome aboard," he said in a cordial tone. "May I see your ticket?"

The silver nameplate on his prim white smock read "Adrian Wills."

Erin handed him her ticket. He studied it briefly, then handed it back. "Your berth is ready, ma'am, please follow me. He took her case and moved back up the aisle. He stopped at a curtain with the number "two" sewn in black thread. Parting the curtain, he placed the small case on the bed of her lower berth.

"The dining car is the next one forward if you would like some dinner before retiring. If you need anything, just push the buzzer in your berth. I'm available anytime during the trip and will be happy to help you," he said with a pleasant smile and returned to his work.

Deciding to freshen up, Erin headed for the women's lounge. She wished her berth had been closer to that end of the car. Afterward, she moved back up the aisle, left her vanity case in the berth and headed for the vestibule that separated her sleeper and dining car. The upper half of the passenger access door was open, filling the confined space with humidity and noise from a myriad of arriving and departing trains. When the dining car door closed behind her, its atmosphere was dry and cool. The outside din was replaced by subdued clinking of tableware and the hum of conversation.

Erin stood for a moment. She looked down the row for an open seat. At the far end an alert steward motioned her to come forward. Moving by other travelers busy with their dinners, she didn't notice the gentleman in a brown suit sitting alone.

"Good evening, Miss," the steward said pulling back a chair.

He asked if she would like something from the bar. Erin ordered a cocktail.

When her drink arrived, she took a taste and studied the menu. After giving her order to a waiter, she realized the dining car had filled and the train had begun to move.

Erin was halfway through her meal when the train rounded a curve. Passengers swayed with the motion. Looking up, she caught a glimpse of someone facing her three tables down. *It's him!* she thought, *that terrible person at the newsstand.* He was seated with someone in a brown suit. She didn't remember either man being there when she entered. It was difficult to see them clearly because their table was on the same side as hers and other diners partially blocked her view. Erin recalled their encounter at the newsstand, and wondered if he had heard her when she called him a jerk. After a moment, Erin realized that her look was so brief that she couldn't be sure it was he. She returned to her meal. As Erin ate, her curiosity remained and occasionally she glanced down the row, but diners still seated in the next two tables prevented her from seeing them.

When Erin finished dinner, she gazed out the window by her table. The evening light had given way to a growing purple sky. She watched as her train passed a highway crossing where red lights flashed at a line of waiting automobiles. Inside the dining car, the warning bells made a muted clanging sound quickly lost by the speeding train. Soon, all that was visible was a faint glimmer of farm lights winking back from the distance.

With little to observe, Erin turned her attention to nearby passengers. The diners two tables down had left, and a couple at the next table were starting to leave. Once they were gone, she could see the man in the brown suit seated with his back to her. He just managed to block her view of the larger man's face. It appeared as if they were having an argument, but Erin was too far away to hear any details of their conversation. Suddenly, the man in the brown suit stood up, threw down his napkin, and hurried into the aisle. He disappeared through the vestibule door. Now she had a clear view, and it *was* the same person she had encountered at the newsstand!

When he looked in her direction, his eyes seemed to glare at her. She felt a wave of panic. *Oh my god! He must know it's me.* Then, as the man motioned with his arm, she realized he was signaling for a waiter.

Relieved, Erin still wondered if he recognized her. If so, he gave no further indication, paid the bill and left without looking her way again. After he was gone, she remembered his chilling look and shuddered. Then she calmed herself. *You're overreacting, Erin. He didn't even notice you,* she thought, hoping she was right.

After paying the bill, Erin left her table and moved toward the vestibule. With the upper exit door still open, a night wind swirled around whipping at her hair. Above the roar, she could hear the train's steel wheels clicking cadence as they sped over the tracks below.

As she entered her coach, Erin noticed the porter had lowered the lighting. The long row of heavy green curtains greeted her in a dim stillness. Feeling the strain of a long day, she checked her watch. It was a little before nine. In Michigan, it would be almost ten. There was no sound from the upper berth as she grabbed her cosmetic case and headed for the women's lounge. Passing the private compartment in the narrow hall, she wondered if someone was sleeping behind the closed door.

Back in her berth, gently rocked by the moving train, she read only two pages of her Readers' Digest before falling asleep.

* * *

5

Traces of light filtered in round the edges of heavy window shades in Erin's berth. She rolled toward the glow and squinted at her wristwatch. It was 6:15a.m.. Lying back, she listened. It was still. Then she realized there was no motion. The train was not moving. Propped up on one elbow, she raised one of the two shades just enough to see out. Blinded by the bright sunshine, she turned away to give her eyes a minute to adjust. She looked out again and could see a sign hanging from the railroad station's eave. It read "FORT DODGE."

Wide-awake, Erin struggled with her robe then pulled back the curtain and stepped out onto the carpeted aisle. Taking her clothes and cosmetic case, she headed for the women's lounge. In the narrow hallway, the conductor and a man in a khaki uniform were standing by the private compartment. As she approached, they stopped their hushed conversation and closed the partially open door. She was greeted by the conductor, "Good morning, ma'am." Erin returned his greeting with a nod as the two men moved against the wall, making room for her to pass. She noticed a shoulder patch on the officer's uniform that read "Webster County Sheriff's Department."

In the lounge, Erin filled a stainless-steel basin with warm water and wondered what had happened that would require the presence of local authorities. Obviously, they were concealing something inside the private compartment.

When she finished dressing, the train was still not moving. Erin's curiosity was tugging at her. She wanted to inquire without being too obvious. Back up the narrow hallway, she questioned the conductor, "Excuse me. Why are we waiting so long at this station?"

"Fort Dodge is a regular stop, ma'am. We're held up loading mail. It shouldn't be long now."

Erin wanted to probe further, but she had enough experience with background work on crime cases to know the authorities would disclose very little during an investigation.

Back at her berth she dropped off the cosmetic case and headed for the dining car. The vestibule passenger door was completely open giving access to the steps. Adrian, the porter, was standing nearby on the platform. Changing her mind, she moved down and inquired if there was time to get a paper.

"Yes, ma'am. It may be a while. Just listen for a couple of loud whistles. It will signal when the train is ready to leave."

"Do you know why we are waiting so long?"

"Not sure, ma'am. I think we are holding the train for someone."

Erin thanked him and walked toward the station. *Maybe you should check with the conductor. He thinks they're busy loading mail!*

On the platform she stopped and drew a deep breath in the fresh air. The sky was a clear liquid blue that appeared as if it went on forever. It was a magnificent spring morning, the first week in June.

Inside at the newsstand, she bought a local paper and noticed two uniformed deputies in conversation as they stood near the lunch counter. Casually, she strolled close enough to hear their exchange and picked up a menu. She pretended to look it over.

A tall gangly deputy was talking to a shorter one. "Yeah, they're holding for some FBI guy from Des Moines. It appears someone had been killed on the train last night."

Whoa! Someone killed in that private compartment while I was sleeping? Maybe it's good my berth is at the other end of the car, she thought.

"Why bring in the FBI?" the shorter deputy asked.

"Interstate transportation is federal jurisdiction."

"Oh, right," the shorter deputy responded, trying to sound like he had known but just forgot.

"Our dispatcher told me the conductor called in from Waterloo. We're supposed to hold the train until the agent gets here."

The deputy had said "killed," but Erin wondered if he meant "murdered." Someone murdered in the same sleeping car made her a little unnerved as she conjured up an image from a recent Bogart movie.

Boarding the train, she went directly to the dining car and requested a table where she could view the station.

She felt it bizarre to have someone killed during the trip when a waiter broke into her thoughts, "Good morning, ma'am. Would you like to start with coffee?"

"Yes, please," Still mulling over the possibilities of what had happened last night, Erin gazed out of her window.

She saw the tall deputy from the lunch counter and a man in a business suit emerge from the station. They moved quickly across the platform and stopped briefly to talk with the conductor. Then all three men walked toward the train and disappeared from her view. At once, the train began to move from the station. *Well, they finally loaded the mail…*

* * *

When Erin returned to her sleeping car, Adrian had transformed her berth into seats for daytime travel with enough space to accommodate four people. She would have plenty of room since the person in the upper berth had apparently departed the train at Fort Dodge.

The Hawkeye was speeding again, passing vast fields of corn with their young leaves bathing in morning sunlight.

A while later, the man she had observed with the conductor interrupted her reading. He appeared to be in his early fifties, trim and well-dressed in a conservative suit. "Good morning, Miss Hays."

It surprised Erin that he knew her name.

"Yes?"

"I'm Ted Gilbert with the Federal Bureau of Investigation," he said. Reaching inside his coat, he produced a small pocket-size folder containing his picture and credentials. "May I sit down?"

"Of course, what is it?" she asked.

He took the seat opposite her. "I would like to ask you a few questions."

"Okay."

"Did you see or hear anything unusual last evening or during the night?"

"In what way?"

"Well, anything out of the ordinary. Other passengers acting in a strange or aggressive manner?"

Erin thought about the man in the brown suit and the big jerk. She had never heard any of their conversation and only guessed there had been an argument. She was not about to tell this FBI agent that she didn't like the looks of the man who had bumped her arm in Chicago.

"No," Erin answered. "I went to the dining car soon after boarding. Later I returned to the sleeping car, changed clothes in the women's lounge and went directly to my berth. It was around nine."

"When you passed the private compartment, did you see anyone going in or out or hear anything?"

"No, it was quiet." She watched as he took notes in a small spiral pad.

" Please take my card and give me a call if you remember something later."

"I will," she answered. "What happened last night that prompted your investigation?" Erin couldn't resist asking.

The agent paused and then gave her a reassuring look. "Nothing to be concerned about, Miss Hays. Just routine. Everything is fine."

A good answer, Mr. Gilbert, she thought.

"Is there a telephone number where you can be contacted?" he asked.

Erin reached for her purse, to look for her address book. She wrote down the Taylor's number on the back of a business card and gave it to him.

"Thank you for your time," he said, standing.

Erin placed his card in her purse, unaware that she would be using it soon.

* * *

6

A repeating wail of the Hawkeye's whistle signaled its approach to Cherokee. When the station came into view, Erin felt excitement growing to see her grandparents again. It had been seven years since her last visit, the summer before she entered law school. It seemed as if she were turning back the calendar to a more promising time in her life.

Through the train window, Erin could see her grandparents standing next to each other on the platform. She remembered as a little girl they had reminded her of two lovable bears because of their rotund appearance.

Adrian was working his way down the aisle to help passengers with their luggage. She rose from her seat and followed along as he placed Erin's cosmetic case near the vestibule steps. Erin handed him three dollars. She wondered if the gratuity for the trip was enough.

He gave her a wide, beaming smile and slipped the bills into his pocket in one smooth motion. "Thank you ma'am. It was a pleasure having you with us." By his enthusiastic response, she assumed her tip was sufficient.

Stepping down from the coach, she moved to meet her grandparents. Erin waived to them, not sure they would recognize her after so long.

"There she is!" Florence Taylor called out, excited at seeing their only grandchild again. They met with a flurry of hugs and exclamations of how wonderful she looked. Bert Taylor, Erin's grandfather, beamed; he could see that she had matured into a very attractive young woman.

"Our granddaughter has become a real lady," he said, observing her with a broad smile.

"I'm sorry the train was late," Erin said.

"No problem. We were a little late ourselves," Florence responded.

Bert took Erin's cosmetic case and followed the two women as they walked, arms linked, across the brick platform.

Her grandparents looked just the same as they had at her last visit. They were still heavy from years of ample farm meals. Their gray hair set off rosy cheeks and sharp clear eyes. Bert's face had more lines and was darker after years in the fields. He looked the part of a man who had earned his living from hard work. Apart from their weight, Erin marveled at how well they seemed for a couple in their early seventies.

"It's such a lovely morning. Let's wait outside," Florence said, guiding her granddaughter toward a bench in front of the station."

When Erin mentioned that she had checked her suitcase, Florence turned to her husband. "Bert, why don't you get Erin's other case while she and I chat?

"Sure," he said. "Erin, if you'll give me your claim check, I'll wave when I have it and meet you both at the car."

Erin watched him as he disappeared into the station. He moved well for his advanced years. She recalled he would be seventy-two in November, just one week before her own birthday.

After sitting down and smoothing the front of her ankle length cotton dress, Florence commented about talking to Erin's mother.

"I had a call from your mother yesterday,"

"Oh?"

"It was a surprise when she told us about her plans to marry again."

Erin had wondered how her grandparents would respond to the news.

"Yes, she told me about it when I visited with her in Kalamazoo. I knew that she and Dr. Paul were good friends, but when she broke the news, it was quite a surprise."

"Your father was a fine man, and I know it must be lonely for her living without him these last few years. It's good to know she is happy and excited about her new life."

Erin was glad to hear that they approved. With the topic of marriage, Erin began to brace herself for a comment on her own prospects, but Gram never mentioned the subject.

"How was your train trip?"

"It was fine. I had a good meal in the dining car last evening and slept well in the berth. We did have some excitement during the night. It's the reason the train was late."

"What happened?" Florence asked, noticing Bert waving at them from the station door. "Oh, excuse me dear, I see Bert has your case."

They rose and began walking toward the parking lot.

"Sorry, please go on."

"When I woke up this morning, we were stopped at Fort Dodge. During the delay, I went into the station and overheard two sheriffs' deputies talking. The authorities were holding our train for a federal agent coming to check on someone who was killed during the night."

"You mean on your train?" Florence asked, wide-eyed.

"Yes."

"Well, for heaven sakes!" Florence exclaimed as they joined her husband. "Bert, you won't believe what Erin just told me! Someone was killed on her train last night!"

Bert looked surprised but didn't say anything as he opened the Buick's trunk to deposit Erin's cases. When they climbed into the car, Florence took the backseat. She told Erin to sit up front.

As they drove away, Florence continued to voice her concern about the incident. "Was it an accident of some kind?"

Erin told them she didn't know how the person had died, but it apparently happened in the sleeping car's only private compartment. "A sheriff's deputy in the station said 'killed,' so there might have been some foul play involved." From the front seat, Erin couldn't see the expression on her grandmother's face, but her tone said she was upset by this added news.

"You mean it happened in the same car where you were sleeping?"

"My berth was at the far end. I wouldn't have known about it except for the deputy's comments," Erin said, trying to quell her grandmother's concern.

"Well, things like this are just terrible." It was plain that Gram did not want any further discussion on the subject, especially if a killing happened near her granddaughter.

There were no more comments about the episode during their twenty-five mile trip to the Taylor's farm. Gram did ask about Erin's life in Detroit and her work at the law firm. Erin kept her news positive telling about the Beck case in court the week before. She had never told them about her engagement to Terry Warner and was glad they didn't know what had happened.

* * *

When they approached the farm, Erin could see the large stucco and brick two-story farmhouse that had been in the Taylor family for three generations. Like most farm homes, the house sat back from the road in a grove. Years before, when the first farmers cleared the land, they left trees near their houses and outbuildings. It provided relief during the summer heat and protection from drifting snow in the winter. The Taylors' land covered more than six hundred acres and was one of the largest farms in the county. Bert employed three full-time hands and hired extra help at harvest-time.

As they moved down the lane, Erin noticed there was a new building off to one side of the farmyard just past the house.

"I see you have added something."

"Yes," Gram answered. "Your grandfather and his men were busy building a new garage most of last winter. Inside, there's a knotty pine paneled office with heat, electricity, and even an extension to our house phone. The way he talks about it, you'd think it's the eighth wonder of the world. To be honest, I'm glad they built it. Keeps him from cluttering up my kitchen with his paperwork."

Bert smiled at his wife's comments as he parked the car in the garage next to a late model Ford pickup truck.

Erin followed her grandfather as he carried her two cases into the house and upstairs to the back guestroom. "There you are. Make yourself at home. I'll be in the garage if you need anything. Just give a yell."

As Erin unpacked, she looked around the cheery corner room with its yellow flowered wallpaper that picked up colors in an oval braided rug. She recalled how morning sunlight flooded the room from an eastern window. Brushing aside the cotton curtains, she looked out at a big red barn and the vast acres of bright green fields.

When her suitcase was empty and everything put away, she removed her clothes, slipped on a robe, then headed for the hall bathroom. The spray from a wide showerhead washed away any thought of two days traveling without a bath. When Erin was ready to wash her hair, she saw a bottle of shampoo on a shelf by the tub and remembered leaving hers at the house in Kalamazoo.

Back in the bedroom, she put on a cream colored cotton blouse, her new tan walking shorts, and a pair of Capri flats. While dressing, she noticed the framed photograph from her mother's wedding on the chest of drawers. Martha was in a white gown with a long train standing next to Erin's father. On each side were Bert and Florence, and everyone was smiling.

They all look so young, she thought, knowing the photograph was more than thirty years old. It was too bad that her father's parents had not lived to see their youngest son married.

The picture reminded her that she had promised to call her mother.

* * *

7

When Erin entered the kitchen, Gram was busy fixing lunch. There were only two plates on the table.

"Where is everyone?" Erin asked.

"I usually feed the men at noon, but Bert sent Hank and Sven into town for something. Sonny was over helping a neighbor this morning and most likely ate his lunch with them. Bert said he had work to do, so I made two sandwiches and a healthy piece of pie. He took them out to his office in the garage. Your grandfather loves it out there with his radio; he even has a hot plate to heat soup or coffee. At times it's like that office is his second home," Florence said, shaking her head.

"Gram, I need to call Mother and let her know that I'm here. Mind if I use the telephone?"

"Heavens no! Use it any time, dear. It's still in the same place in the hall. Do you recall what to do? Just take the receiver off the hook and turn the crank. The local operator will come on the line. Tell her you want long-distance."

"Yes, I remember. Would you like to talk to Mom?"

"No, just give her our best. When she called yesterday, we talked for a spell."

Erin gave the wall telephone crank three good turns.

The conversation with her mother was brief. Voices on the long-distance call were weak, because of the country party line, and not conducive to long conversations. Martha was glad to hear that her daughter had arrived safely, and Erin didn't mention the incident on the train. Gram's being upset was enough.

When Erin returned to the kitchen Gram was at the table waiting for her. "I hope you still like cold chicken sandwiches. I made the potato salad this morning before we left."

"That sounds fine," Erin said.

Florence Taylor was an excellent cook. With little effort, she could whip up enough food to feed ten hungry farmhands. "If you'd like some dessert, I made an apple pie last evening."

"Easy, Gram. You know I love your cooking, but I only brought one size of clothing."

"You need to put some meat on those bones of yours, girl. You always were too skinny."

Erin's only response was to take a bite of the delicious chicken sandwich.

Near the end of their meal, Florence again asked about her granddaughter's work at the law firm. Erin wanted to be as candid as she could without bringing up the reason behind her visit and the concern with her career. "I've been working hard, putting in long hours, and I needed to take a break. I felt a couple of weeks here at the farm with you and Gramps would be a pleasant vacation."

Gram shook her head in amazement. "It seems the war has changed everything. I figured that when it was over, women doing men's work would go back to the way it was. If they don't, who will stay home and raise the family?"

Erin didn't say anything. Her only response was to shrug her shoulders rather than debate the issue with her grandmother.

"Anyway, it's great to have you visit with us again. You're welcome to stay as long as you like. Now, how about some pie?"

Erin seldom ate desserts, especially at the noon meal, but she was glad that Gram had changed the subject and accepted the offer. When the last crumb was gone, Erin asked if they would need the car this afternoon. She wanted to pick up something in Parkston.

"I left my shampoo at mother's. Would it be all right if I borrowed the Buick?

"Sure, dear. Just take it when you're ready. I hardly ever drive myself, and Bert always uses the pickup. You'll find the keys are either on the hook by the kitchen door or in the car."

Erin thought that in Detroit she would never leave her keys in the car.

When Erin entered the new building through an open garage door, she walked past the Buick and Ford pickup. She paused at the entrance to Gramps' office. Through a window in the door, she could see Bert was sitting at a large rolltop desk. He was talking to someone in coveralls. The familiar looking man sat in a sturdy wooden chair and had it tilted back against the wall. When she opened the door, both men looked in her direction.

"Well, here she is, Sonny! You returned just in time to meet Erin. You remember my granddaughter?" Bert asked beaming with a look of pride.

"Yes, I do," the man answered, quickly dropping his chair back onto four legs. He stood up and removed his frayed baseball cap. "Nice to see you again, Miss Hays."

"It's good to see you, Sonny. Please sit down; don't let me interrupt anything."

He returned to the chair and appeared shy in the presence of Bert's attractive granddaughter. Sonny was tall and lean, weathered from a lifetime of summers in the sun. In his mop of dishwater blond hair, there where strands of gray. He appeared older than his forty-two years.

"I see you changed your clothes. Are you settled in?" Bert asked.

"Yes, I had lunch with Gram. She said it would be all right to borrow the Buick. I need to pick up something in town. Thought I should check with you."

"Sure, take it anytime. It should have plenty of gas. I filled it up before we left for the trip to Cherokee."

"Thanks. I shouldn't be too long." As she closed the office door, Erin could see through the window that Sonny had replaced his cap and tilted the chair back against the wall.

In the car she adjusted the seat and rearview mirror, then drove out the lane and turned north on the county road.

Taylors' farm was four miles from the small town of Parkston. She drove three miles on gravel county roads, one more on US 59, the concrete highway that ran past the east side of town. Parkston was the seat of O'Brien County and had a population of just over nine hundred.

Ten minutes later, Erin pulled Taylors' sedan into a diagonal parking space in front of the town's drugstore. Across a wide brick street was the county courthouse, a massive stone building surrounded on all sides by a deep lawn and mature trees. It was Parkston's largest building and stood in the center of the town square.

When Erin entered the drugstore, a girl in her middle teens was behind a soda counter. "Hello," she said, "can I help you with something?"

"Yes, I need some shampoo," Erin responded.

"It's down the far aisle on the right. Let me show you." The young clerk moved ahead of Erin and stopped at a display of hair products. While Erin looked for the brand she wanted, the girl studied Erin's stylish walking shorts. She had seen them in a recent fashion magazine.

"Do you live in the area?" she asked.

"No, just visiting. My grandparents are the Taylors. It's been some time since my last visit."

The girl brightened. "I remember Mrs. Taylor talking about her granddaughter, a successful lawyer with a big firm in Detroit! Are you the one?" she asked, seeming pleased at recalling the conversation with Erin's grandmother.

"Well, I'm an attorney. The successful part is questionable."

The girl seemed impressed. "I never met a lady attorney. Do you attend court and talk in front of a judge and a jury?"

"Yes, when I'm involved in a case that goes to trial."

"Wow! That sounds really exciting! Are you called a lawyer, or is it attorney?"

"Either one is fine. Attorneys are legally empowered to act for another. If they represent someone in court, they're called lawyers."

The young clerk continued to stay by Erin's side, captivated as if in the presence of a celebrity.

Finding what she wanted, Erin paid for the item and thanked the young woman for her help. As she climbed into the Buick, Erin could see the girl smiling and waving at her from the front window.

When Erin reached the highway, a sheriff's patrol car with its red lights flashing raced by, heading south out of town. After it passed, she turned in the same direction heading back to the farm. Far down the road, the speeding patrol car disappeared over a small hill.

As Erin crested the rise, she saw red flares some distance ahead on the pavement. Two patrol cars with their emergency lights still flashing, were parked across both lanes blocking the highway on each side of a large wrecker. Slowing near the scene, she could make out a large tractor-trailer still upright but down in a ditch on her side of the road.

As Erin stopped a safe distance from the patrol car, she could see three men standing on the pavement. Two official appearing men in khaki clothes were talking to a third man in jeans and a faded blue work shirt.

After a while, one of the men noticed her car and walked over. Other than his khaki shirt and pants, he wore boots and a western style straw hat. The man stopped by her open driver's side window and looked in. Erin could see the word "Sheriff" on the gold star pinned to his shirt. When he spoke, his clear gray eyes held her attention. They were friendly but strangely penetrating.

"Sorry, ma'am, you'll have to wait a while until we can get the road clear."

"What happened?" She asked, captivated for the moment by the intensity of his steady gaze.

"The driver pulled his rig off the pavement to check a loose trailer door. Soft earth on the shoulder gave way under his truck's weight, forcing him down into the ditch. It was lucky he didn't tip over. We should have it back on the road soon."

For an instant, she had the odd feeling as if something passed between them.

He nodded, smiled, and walked away.

After a time, the big semi was still not moving. The tow truck operator had to unhook and reposition for better leverage.

The afternoon's summer sun began to heat the car's interior, so Erin opened her door and stepped outside. She never gave a thought to how she looked with her slim silhouette leaning against the sedan. The breeze tossed her auburn hair.

It wasn't long before the sheriff returned. "This looks like Bert Taylor's Buick. Are you his granddaughter?"

"Yes, I'm staying with them for a while."

The sheriff removed his straw hat and wiped his forehead with a shirt sleeve. His sandy blond hair was thin on top for someone who looked to be not much beyond thirty. He was at least six feet tall and handsome with a strong, rugged appearance. From the way he carried himself, she sized him up as someone who was comfortable with being in charge.

Erin was about to say something when noise from the tow truck's wheels spinning wildly against the concrete roadway stopped her. Blue smoke and the odor of burned rubber filled the air as the tractor-trailer slowly began to ease back toward the pavement.

"Everything should be clear in a moment, Miss Hays. It was a pleasure meeting you," he said and quickly headed toward his cruiser. In a few minutes, the sheriff and his deputy moved their patrol units, opening one lane to traffic.

Erin slid behind the wheel and pulled her car around the mud-splattered livestock rig and continued south toward the county road turnoff.

As Erin drove, she thought about the sheriff, the way he looked at her, and recalled he had never mentioned his name.

* * *

8

That evening, Florence Taylor was busy placing huge portions of food on the table. She called upstairs to her husband, "Supper is ready, Bert. Don't let it get cold!"

"I'm coming. Don't get your skirt in a flutter," he hollered back just before bursting into the kitchen and taking a seat across from his granddaughter. There was enough food in front of him to feed half a dozen hungry field hands. "Looks good!" Bert said, tucking a napkin in his shirtfront. "I'm really hungry tonight."

"I don't remember a night when you weren't," his wife answered.

"How was your trip to town, Erin?" she asked, while passing her granddaughter a large bowl of steaming mashed potatoes.

"Fine. The town hasn't changed much since my last visit."

"They're talking about turning the old Houston Hotel into apartments. The place has been empty, gathering dust since they closed four years ago," Bert chimed in while helping himself to a sizable chunk of pot roast.

"There was a little excitement on my way back home this afternoon," Erin commented. "A tractor-trailer had run off the highway. The road was blocked in both directions, so I had to wait while a large wrecker was attempting to pull it back on the pavement. The sheriff was there. He recognized your car and surprised me when he knew who I was."

"So, you met our local hero," Bert said, pouring a stream of hot gravy over everything on his plate. "He was badly wounded during the invasion of France while saving his entire company from a German ambush."

"Now, Bert, I don't think the paper said it was his entire company," Florence broke in, trying to temper her husband's enthusiastic version.

"No matter," Bert continued. "He was in a military hospital back east for some months recovering from his surgery. While he was there, his fiancée left him and ran off to California. When he returned home, the town had a big celebration. They even had the governor over from Des Moines to welcome him back. Later, he ran for Sheriff and easily won the election with the biggest margin in our county's history. He's a likable fellow. Everyone around here respects him."

"Your sheriff sounds like someone rather special," Erin said, recalling the moment when their eyes had met. "We didn't talk long. It was noisy when the truck came out of the ditch, and he never mentioned his name."

"Robert Thomas," Gram said, passing a bowl of snap beans to Bert. "I saved the local paper about his being wounded. When I find it, I'll leave it in your room."

"Thanks," Erin said.

When it was time for dessert, Erin couldn't resist and had another piece of Gram's wonderful apple pie. When the last bite disappeared from her plate, Erin was so full she felt as if she wouldn't eat again for a week.

Tired from the long trip, Erin was in bed early that night. She slept soundly as cool air flowed through the open windows. During the early morning hours, she began to roll and mumble in her sleep, dreaming she was back in the Hawkeye dining car with the waiter serving unending dishes of food. The dream began to fade as she heard a strange twittering sound. Squinting through sleepy eyes, Erin realized morning sun was flooding the room. In the grove, birds were busy talking back and forth.

* * *

Downstairs, Florence was busy at the sink cleaning vegetables when Erin shuffled in. "Good morning, dear. How did you sleep?" Gram asked.

"Fine, just not awake." Erin pulled her robe tight as a draft blew in through an open kitchen window. She yawned then sat down at the table. Last night's dream had all but faded from her memory.

"What time is it, Gram?" she asked.

"Five after seven," her grandmother replied.

"I guess the train trip tired me more than I thought. I slept nearly nine hours."

"Well, my dear, are you ready for breakfast? Your grandfather had his more than two hours ago."

"Just some toast and coffee will be fine," Erin said. She could see that Gram had everything ready to fix a big breakfast, but she was still feeling full from the night before. "What is Gramps doing this morning?"

"He's been trying to call Ed Lawrence, our neighbor on the farm just south of us. Bert has been working with him to lease some of his land. Ed was on a trip and may not be back yet."

"Where did he go?" Erin asked, sipping from a large mug of hot coffee.

"I'm not sure. Bert thinks he should be back by now. He might be outside and can't hear the phone. A strange man if you ask me, living on that place of his all by himself."

The sound of the rear porch screen door slamming shut announced the arrival of Bert as he entered the kitchen. "Good morning there, young lady! How did you sleep?" he asked, placing an empty thermos bottle on the table.

"Good morning, Gramps. I slept just fine. A little chilly this morning, though." Erin had her hands wrapped around the hot coffee cup, savoring its warmth.

Florence moved to the stove, filled her husband's thermos, then set it back on the table. "Are you still going over to check on Ed?" she asked.

"Yes, I need to settle this issue about leasing those forty acres. Joe said if we want to start plowing over there, I need to get the papers signed." He looked at Erin. "You may not remember Joe Butler. He's our attorney."

"He's just about everybody's attorney, being the only one in Parkston," Florence added.

Bert picked up his newly filled thermos and headed toward the rear porch when he stopped. "Erin, would you like to ride along while I go over to the Lawrence place?"

"Oh, Bert, let her be. She just got up and hasn't had any breakfast."

Erin was sure that her grandmother was trying to keep her at the table, hoping she would eat something.

"Yes, I would. Do I have time to change into my clothes?"

"No rush. Take all the time you need," Bert said, heading out the back door.

* * *

Erin quickly made the bed, brushed her teeth, and tied her hair back with a ribbon. She pulled on a pair of jeans, a blouse, and tennis shoes, then headed back downstairs.

"You look just like that young college girl who was here the last time," Gram said, clearing the table.

Erin laughed. "Thanks Gram. It feels great to be back with you and Gramps again." It pleased Erin that Gram was not fussing about her skipping breakfast, but her grandmother was not one to give up easily.

"Here, dear, take this along in case you feel hungry. I don't know how you keep going with so little food in you." She handed her granddaughter a small brown paper bag containing two huge berry muffins and a napkin.

Erin started to protest, then decided it would be best just to take them. "No one will starve when you're around, Gram." Then telling her grandmother "goodbye." She headed out the kitchen door.

Bert was putting down the phone's receiver when Erin entered his office. "Still no answer at Ed's place. Let's go ahead and drive over there. What's in the paper sack?"

"Gram thinks I might not make the trip without more food. So she gave me some muffins."

Her grandfather chuckled. "Florence has fixed so many meals over the years she just doesn't feel right unless she's feeding someone. How do you think I got this big?"

* * *

"I don't remember this Mr. Lawrence," Erin said as Bert drove the pickup south along the county road.

44

"He showed up about four years ago," Bert explained. "You might remember the farm used to be the old Madison place."

"No, I don't recall anyone who lived there," Erin said.

"Well, anyway, Ed is like a hermit. Lives alone with his dog. The farm has nearly two hundred acres, and he has never planted any crops. The fields are just growing into weeds. I've been trying to lease forty acres from him for soybeans. It's taken me nearly all winter getting him to come around. When he finally agreed, I had Joe Butler work up a lease and mail him a copy. We planned to meet yesterday afternoon to sign it when he got back."

"Why would he buy a property with all that land and then not farm it?"

"That's a good question. The talk is he doesn't even have a mortgage on the place. Bought it from the bank a year after Jed Madison died. They say he just wrote a check for the full amount."

"Sounds like the man is rather wealthy."

"Ed pays cash for everything he buys. The strange part is he is some kind of war refugee. He told me he was from some little town in Switzerland. Sometimes I can hardly understand him. Has a real strong accent."

"I thought that most war refugees were poor," Erin said.

"Your grandmother's cousin Sadie still works part-time at the bank. She told Florence on the quiet that she is sure he has a safety deposit box filled with cash."

Erin shook her head. "Sounds like he doesn't trust people."

Bert turned the pickup off the county road onto a dirt farm lane that curved through a grove of trees. "Is this it?" Erin asked.

"Yep, secluded isn't it?"

"I guess so. You can't see much from the road. If a silo wasn't showing above the treetops, you'd never know anything was back there. The guy must like his privacy."

Bert drove through the trees and stopped in the farmyard.

Erin could see the house and outbuildings were in good repair and nicely painted. "His place looks well cared for," she said.

"Madison had been ill for some time before he died, leaving everything in rather bad shape. After Lawrence bought it, he must have spent plenty fixing up the house and livestock buildings he never uses," Bert said, starting to open his door.

"Why don't you wait here in case the dog is loose."

"If you don't mind, I want to tag along. You've got my curiosity aroused about Mr. Lawrence. Besides, I've always liked dogs."

They left the pickup and walked over to a screened-in rear porch. Bert climbed the steps, opened the screen door and moved to the kitchen entrance. He knocked a few times then waited. There was no response. Erin could hear muffled barking from across the farmyard.

"Rolf must still be shut in," Bert said. Together he and Erin headed for the barn. "I agreed we would look after him while Ed was gone this week. We let Rolf loose during the day, and I usually have one of the men put him back in at night. He's still young, just over a year old. He's a big one. Eats like a horse."

As they approached, the barking became more intense. "Better stay back until he calms down. Once he knows it's me, he should be all right." Bert opened the top half of access to the cream separator room. When the dog recognized him, his barking turned to excited yelps. "Just hold still so he knows you're not a threat," Bert cautioned. When the bottom half of the door was open, the big shepherd bolted out. After a couple of quick sniffs at the female stranger, he ran straight for his bowl by the back porch steps. Finding it empty, he bounded back, barking for his morning meal.

"Ed gives him the run of the farm. Rolf lets him know if anybody is nosing around. When I first pulled in after Lawrence got the dog, he kept me inside my pickup until Ed came out and ran him off."

"It doesn't look like Mr. Lawrence cares for visitors," Erin offered. Then she asked about the Shepherd's name. "I don't remember hearing of a dog called *Rolf*."

"I never heard it before either. Lawrence told me it's a German word for *wolf*. Guess Ed could have gone to town, but it doesn't look like it with his dog still in the barn and doesn't seem like he's been fed. I'll feed him, and we might as well go."

"Let me do it, Gramps. It will give us a chance to make friends."

"Go ahead. While you do that, I'll check the front of the house."

Erin found two large bags of dog chow on the porch. One was open and mostly full. She lugged it down the steps and began to fill his large bowl. The shepherd saw what she was doing and came running. He began devouring his food before she could finish pouring it.

"I didn't see any sign that Lawrence is home," Bert said. We can let the dog run loose, and I'll come over later this evening and put him in the barn if Ed hasn't returned."

* * *

On the way home, Erin asked Gramps about Lawrence's trip.

"He left last Sunday. Said he would back no later than Friday ."

"You seem surprised that he hasn't returned yet."

"Ed is very set in his routine. It's just doesn't seem like him."

As they returned home and pulled into the garage, she handed him the paper sack of muffins. "Please keep these in your office. I don't want Gram to think I didn't appreciate her caring about me."

"No problem, I may get hungry and eat them myself."

"Thanks, Gramps," she said, amazed at his appetite.

When Erin entered the house, her grandmother was at her usual place in the kitchen. "Well, what did you two find out? "

"Mr. Lawrence wasn't there and no sign that he had returned. His dog was still in the barn. Gramps said if Lawrence had returned, Rolf would have been loose. We fed him and left."

"I don't know why your grandfather thinks Ed should have been back just because of those lease papers. I'm sure he'll show up in a day or two."

Erin's mind had been on something else as she watched her grandmother put a beef roast in the oven. "Have you and Gramps thought about going back east to Mom's wedding?"

"Not really. I would like to go. We haven't been anywhere for ages, but October is harvest-time, and it will be the devil getting Bert to leave."

"I know it would make mother happy if you can make it," Erin said.

* * *

At the noon meal, Erin watched in awe as Gramps downed second and third helpings. She wondered if he had eaten the muffins.

Afterward, Gram agreed to let Erin help clear up the kitchen. Once the dishes were clean and put away, her grandmother shooed Erin out of the kitchen.

Upstairs in her room, Erin saw the newspaper on the dresser that

Gram had mentioned at supper the night before. Taking a chair by the window, she unfolded the late, June, 1944 weekly issue of the *O'Brien County Bell* and immediately noticed the bold headline:

LOCAL MAN D-DAY HERO

Captain Robert Leo Thomas, Commander of Baker Company in the 101ˢᵗ Airborne Division, received the Silver Star for saving a platoon of his men pinned down by German machine gun fire during the Normandy invasion on June sixth. Captain Thomas also received the Purple Heart, being seriously wounded during the action. He is recovering from surgery at a military hospital in London, England.

Captain Thomas was a graduate of Parkston High School and received a bachelor's degree from the University of Iowa in the spring of 1941. Following the tragedy at Pearl Harbor, he enlisted in the military and completed training at Fort Bragg, North Carolina, in late 1942. The army assigned him to a ranger unit in North Africa where he received a battle field commission as a second lieutenant. Captain Thomas is the only son of the late Wilber and Gwen Thomas. No additional information on his status was available at press time.

* * *

Late in the afternoon, Erin was walking in the grove when she heard the sound of an automobile turning into the farm. Through the trees, she could see a patrol car stopping near the back porch.

She entered the house and heard voices coming from the living room. Bert and Florence were sitting on a couch in front of the room's bay window, while Sheriff Thomas was in a wingback chair facing them. His straw hat was perched on one knee.

"Here she is," Bert said. "Have a seat, Erin. I think you two met on the highway yesterday."

"Hello, Miss Hays," he said, standing as she entered.

"Hello, Sheriff. Please, sit down."

His manner was polite but more formal than it had been at the accident sight.

"Let me get everyone coffee or iced tea, maybe some cookies," Florence offered.

"I'm fine, Mrs. Taylor. I won't be staying long," the sheriff responded. The look on his face was serious. "I'm afraid that I have some bad news about your neighbor, Edward Lawrence." The room was silent. "He was killed on the train from Chicago last Thursday night."

Florence Taylor gasped. "Oh, no! He must have been the man you told us about, Erin! This is just terrible!"

The deep frown on Bert Taylor's face expressed his shock at the news. He stared at Sheriff Thomas in disbelief.

The sheriff continued. "I had a call from Ted Gilbert. He's an agent with the FBI in Des Moines. He mentioned interviewing Erin last Friday morning on the train and would like to meet with her again."

"Oh, Erin, what would they want with you?"

"It's fine, Gram. They interviewed everyone. Now that they have identified Mr. Lawrence, they are just following up for possible leads," Erin said, hoping to reassure her grandmother.

The sheriff began again, "Gilbert is planning to be here tomorrow and wants to check out the Lawrence farm after the meeting. He is driving over from Des Moines. He plans to be here around eleven. Could you be in town at my office about that time, Miss Hays?"

"Sure," Erin answered, wondering what Gilbert's concern might be.

Sheriff Thomas stood up, thanked them for their time and expressed his sympathy over the loss of their neighbor.

Bert suggested that, if the sheriff would give him a call before heading to the Lawrence farm, he would put the dog back in the barn.

Everyone moved back to the kitchen. Sheriff Thomas stopped at the rear door and turned to Erin. For a second their eyes met. "I'll see you in the morning then, Miss Hays?" he asked.

"Yes, I'll be there," she answered. He was facing the light, and she could see that his gray eyes contained tiny flecks of blue. For an instant she felt the same sensation as she had yesterday on the highway. Then he was out the door and in his patrol car, quickly disappearing from view.

Erin wondered what he had been thinking when he had looked at her so intensely. Did he consider her a suspect in the Lawrence killing or did his look convey something else?

* * *

Supper that night was quiet. Edward Lawrence's death cast a gloom over their meal. After helping clear the dishes, Erin decided to walk through the pasture down to a small stream that ran through a back section of the farm. Years earlier, her grandfather had built a dam that formed a pond. Soon young willow trees had begun to grow at the water's edge, secluding the place from sight. When she had visited one summer, the pond had been a favorite place to hide out. Once, on an especially hot summer day, she had shed her clothes and frolicked in the cool water. As Erin's thoughts drifted back to that carefree time, it seemed far removed from her current frustration with life in Detroit.

* * *

9

When Erin entered the town square Monday morning, she noticed a late model four-door sedan with Polk County plates was parked in front of the sheriff's office. Erin assumed it was Ted Gilbert's car as she pulled into the empty space beside it.

The combination office and jail was a solitary one-story stone building situated on a corner across from the courthouse. She walked up four granite steps and entered the front door.

Inside, the same deputy who had been at the highway accident on Friday rose from a desk behind the reception counter.

"I'm here to see Sheriff Thomas."

"Yes, Miss Hays. The sheriff is expecting you. His office is just down the hall to the right." He moved to a barrier gate, holding it open for her to pass.

At the partly open door marked "Private," she could see the federal agent and Sheriff Thomas talking. They stopped at the sound of her light knock. Both men stood as she entered.

"Good morning," Gilbert said.

Sheriff Thomas gave her a polite smile, nodded his greeting and motioned toward an empty chair next to the FBI agent.

The office was large but sparingly furnished. Four tall metal filing cabinets and a plain oak table with six straight-back chairs occupied the opposite side of the room. Next to a gun rack on the wall behind the sheriff's gray steel desk, was a large framed photo with five rows of smiling soldiers. It had signatures scrawled all around the borders. Across the bottom margin in bold print were the words "BAKER COMPANY, 101st AIRBORNE."

"I apologize for bringing you out on Sunday, Miss Hays," Gilbert said. "I'm sure you can appreciate the critical timing in a murder case."

It was the first time Erin recalled hearing the word "murder."

"Let's go over everything one more time. Please, start from when you boarded in Chicago."

"I'm sorry, but there isn't much I can tell you that would add to our conversation on the train."

"Please, let's review it anyway," he said.

"After boarding, I freshened up and went directly to the dining car for dinner. Later, I returned to the sleeping car, retrieved my cosmetic case from the berth and changed in the women's lounge. Then I returned to my berth and fell asleep reading."

"When you passed the private compartment did you hear voices or any sounds?" The agent glanced down at the same small spiral pad he had used to make notes that day on the Hawkeye.

"No. As I said that day on the train, it was quiet. I would have noticed any unusual noises."

"Did you see either the porter or the conductor?"

"No, no one."

"What time was it when you returned to your berth from the lounge?"

"It was shortly before nine."

"How did you know the time?" He asked, again checking his notes.

"I remember looking at my watch just after entering the berth."

Erin did not mention seeing either man in the dining car. She had thought about the person with a scar before coming today, but she knew it would be wrong to incriminate someone because of the way he looked, especially when her feelings reflected his rude behavior at the newsstand. Also, she had never seen the face of the man thought to be Edward Lawrence and couldn't identify him.

"Well, thank you for going over it again. If you recall something later please contact me right away."

Erin gave him an understanding look and nodded that she would.

Gilbert turned to the sheriff. "Can we visit the Lawrence Farm now?"

Sheriff Thomas broke his silence with a simple, "Yes."

Erin was sure that while she and Gilbert had been talking, the sheriff hadn't missed anything in their conversation.

When they reached the reception counter, Thomas asked his deputy to call Bert Taylor and let him know they were leaving for the Lawrence place.

"I'd like you to be there also, if you don't mind, Miss Hays. There might be a few more questions," Gilbert said. His tone was friendly but direct.

"That's fine," Erin said, wanting to tag along. Later, as she followed them in the Buick, she was surprised that she was actually enjoying the intrigue surrounding the Taylor's strange neighbor.

* * *

When the trio of autos came to a stop in Ed Lawrence's farmyard, Bert Taylor was already there, standing next to his pickup. After the sheriff introduced Agent Gilbert, Bert mentioned that Lawrence had installed new locks after he had bought the place. Gilbert asked the sheriff if he had been able to get a warrant to search the property, and Thomas confirmed he had.

After sizing up the outbuildings, Agent Gilbert walked to the rear porch steps. Turning to Bert and Erin he said, "I'm sorry, but you two will have to wait outside. There is no telling what we might find, and I want to keep the place as undisturbed as possible."

Erin wanted to see inside the house, but she knew Gilbert was following procedure.

Standing in the farmyard, Erin and her grandfather watched as both men huddled together near the kitchen door. She could hear the sheriff suggesting they break out the lower pane and open the door from the inside.

"That may not be necessary," Gilbert said, reaching into his suit pocket. He produced a small case that contained oddly shaped metal objects. Bending down, he inserted two of them into the key slot, made a few twists, and then turned the knob. The door opened. It impressed

Erin how quickly Gilbert had been able to pick the lock. *Agent Gilbert would make a good second story man,* she thought.

As Erin and her grandfather waited, she could hear Rolf's barking from his seclusion in the barn.

After a short while, the two men returned to the porch. "The place is in order and undisturbed, no sign of anything unusual. The man had quality furnishings, and was surprisingly neat for a bachelor," Gilbert commented. He seemed satisfied at finding the house as Lawrence had apparently left it. The agent then asked Sheriff Thomas if he would have the property posted and checked on routinely.

Before leaving, Gilbert talked with Bert Taylor about his dealings with Edward Lawrence. Bert recounted what he knew about the dead man, including their proposed lease agreement.

When Gilbert felt he had covered everything, he thanked Erin and her grandfather. He apologized again for taking their time on Sunday.

After he and Sheriff Thomas left, Erin told her grandfather she would like to stay long enough to let the dog loose again. Bert agreed and drove off in his pickup. When Erin opened the separator room door, the pent-up shepherd flew out in such a rush he nearly knocked her down. Then, catching sight of a squirrel near the grove, he dashed after it and disappeared into the trees.

For a time, Erin paused and studied the quiet house. Then she left.

* * *

That night, asleep in her bed, Erin dreamed she was back in her berth on the Hawkeye.

In the morning, when Erin awakened, she lay still with her eyes closed trying to remember the details of last night's dream. It had been dark in the berth and there was no movement. Was the train stopped? She rolled toward the window, and pulled back the edge of the shade. Outside fog swirled around a low building with a sign that read; "Water…" she couldn't see it clearly. Then, there was a rustling noise in the aisle, and something brushed her berth curtain. She peeked out and saw someone in a dark suit rush by. Why was the conductor in such a hurry? She struggled to remember what happened as the edges of the apparition kept slipping away. She couldn't see the man clearly because of the narrow aisle and the low position of her berth, at least not until he had entered the vestibule. Then, just as the door started to close an overhead light caught his face, and the vision hit her with a jolt. "Oh my god! It wasn't the conductor running down the aisle. It was him! The man from the news stand."

During her morning shower, Erin suddenly realized what she had recalled was not just a crazy dream but something that had actually happened. Memories of it surfaced while she slept. After toweling off, she hurried down the hall to her room and quickly dressed.

Downstairs, Erin found her grandmother at the kitchen counter rolling out the dough for a pie crust. A bowl of peeled and diced apples nearby. It was 7:30. As usual her grandfather had eaten his breakfast long before.

"Good morning, Gram!" Erin said sounding especially cheerful.

"Well, a good morning to you!" Gram responded. "You're full of spunk today. Did you sleep well?"

"Yes, and I'm quite sure I know who killed Edward Lawrence," Erin said taking a sip of the hot coffee Gram had placed in front of her.

"My goodness, Erin! Why would you think such a thing?"

"I recalled something about that night on the train." Erin didn't want to sound foolish telling her grandmother that it had come to her in a dream.

"I hope this doesn't get you more involved in this awful killing."

"Don't worry, Gram. Passing along what I know should end my part in the matter." Erin thought it best to drop the subject and call Ted Gilbert after breakfast. She changed their conversation to something that would please her grandmother.

"Gram, how about some bacon and eggs? I'm ready for a real country breakfast." It was the right request.

After finishing a meal that would satisfy a hungry field hand, she went up to her room and wrote down everything she could remember about that night on the train then placed a call to Gilbert

The FBI operator in Des Moines said that Agent Gilbert was not available, but she would give him the message as soon as he called in.

Erin had just finished making her bed when she heard the telephone ring the Taylors' party line signal of two short, one long. When Gram called upstairs that it was Mr. Gilbert, Erin grabbed her notes and rushed back down to the hall phone.

"Hello, Mr. Gilbert?"

"Is that you, Miss Hays?"

"Yes, I wanted to let you know that I have some more information that might be helpful."

"Tell me what you have and let's see where it goes."

Over the next few minutes, Erin told Gilbert about the newsstand incident and her seeing the same man in her dining car with someone that could have been Edward Lawrence. When she related that now, she remembered waking up in her berth and recognizing the man with a scar as he rushed by, possibly leaving the train. Erin hoped it sounded credible. Gilbert patiently listened to everything. When she finished, he thanked her for the information and said they would check it out along with other leads in their investigation.

Erin returned to the kitchen and sat down at the table. As she munched on one of Gram's oatmeal cookies, the morning's excitement over her recollection began to ebb. *I hope this wasn't a mistake because of my annoyance over that big jerk at the newsstand,* she thought.

Florence Taylor noticed that after the phone call her granddaughter seemed troubled. "Well, dear, no harm done if it doesn't pan out. At least you did what you felt was right."

* * *

Later in the day, Erin remembered it had been a week since she had left Detroit for Kalamazoo. She decided to give Diane a call.

"Hi, Diane, it's me," Erin said when her secretary came on the line.

"Hey, stranger, how are you? Better yet, where are you? This connection is a little faint," said Diane.

"I'm at my grandparents' in Iowa. What's going on at the firm?"

"Your absence has created quite a stir. All week long there has been a stream of attorneys coming in to pick up case files. A memo came through from upstairs saying that until further notice you would not be available for pretrial work. You should hear the grumbling as they came by for their folders. Your worktable is nearly empty."

"That's good to hear. Anything else going on?"

"Oh, an item of office gossip. Garrett Barton was telling anyone who would listen to him that he had the Beck trial wrapped up before you took over."

"Sounds like he is trying to cover for his drinking," Erin responded.

"Here is the best part. I heard that last Wednesday they called Barton upstairs and Frank Davis gave him a lecture on his behavior and a warning about drinking. Since then, our Mr. Barton has not said another word about the Beck case. Mark one down for our side."

Erin was happy to hear that management was being supportive. She did not want to appear smug, but she wasn't disappointed to hear that Barton had his big mouth silenced for once.

"I had better hang up before you tell me something I don't want to hear," Erin said with a chuckle.

"Well, that is about it here in lawyersville. You enjoy yourself, and let me know if you meet any neat men. We miss you."

Erin thanked her and said she would check back in a few days. After hanging up, she thought about Barton. He had not helped with any of the pretrial work and never appeared in court after the first six jurors had been seated.

* * *

10

On Tuesday morning after breakfast, Erin asked Gram if she could borrow the Buick for a trip into town.

"Go anytime. Bert and all three of the men are down in the south field, and they won't be back 'til noon."

Erin thanked her grandmother and headed for the garage.

In a short while she was in town parked in front of the drugstore. Erin went inside to find something to read and had only been there a short time when a sheriff's deputy came through the front door.

"Have you seen Miss Hays?" he asked the young clerk.

"Yes, she's back by the magazine rack."

The deputy moved quickly down the aisle and stopped as Erin looked up. "Miss Hays, I'm Frank Martin. Sheriff Thomas would like you to come over to our office as soon as possible." There was a sense of urgency in the young man's voice.

"What does he want?" she asked.

"I don't know. Something about a call from the FBI."

"Well, let's not keep the sheriff waiting. Tell him I'll be right over."

Erin drove around Parkston's town square and parked near the sheriff's office.

Robert Thomas was at his desk studying some papers when Erin knocked on the open office door. "Come in," he said.

"What did you want to see me about?" she asked, taking a seat in one of two chairs facing his desk.

"Agent Gilbert called. He tried to reach you at the farm, and Mrs.

Taylor said you should be here in town. I hope Deputy Martin didn't alarm you."

"No, he just seemed eager to let me know about the call."

"Gilbert wants to know if you could be in Des Moines tomorrow."

"What for?"

"I don't know any details, but your information on the Lawrence killing was helpful. He asked to have you call him soon as possible. If you're ready, we can place a call now."

"Fine," she answered.

He depressed a lever on an intercom box. "Sara."

"Yes sir?"

"Please place a call to Agent Gilbert at his office in Des Moines. Let me know as soon as he's on the line."

He released the lever and stood up. Robert suggested that Erin take his place behind the desk where it would be easier to use his phone.

When she was seated, Erin looked at him for some sign of intensity toward her, but there wasn't the same connection as before. She assumed his thoughts were somewhere else or what had occurred between them was simply her imagination.

In a short time, the telephone rang. Robert leaned over his desk and picked up the receiver. "Sheriff Thomas. Yes, she's right here. Just a moment. It's Gilbert for you." He handed Erin the phone.

The agent confirmed that her information had been helpful. If possible they would like her in Des Moines to go through some files. Tomorrow, if she could. Gilbert said he would ask the sheriff to have someone drive her over. When she agreed, he asked to talk with the sheriff again.

Erin handed the telephone back across the desk. "He wants to speak to you."

"Yes, I understand. We'll see that she gets there sometime late in the morning."

He hung up the telephone and sat back in the chair. For a long moment, he sat quietly, deep in thought.

"Is there a problem?" she asked.

"No, it's just that I'm shorthanded with one man on vacation."

"I can drive myself if it's a problem," she said. "I'm sure my grandparents would let me use their car."

"No, this case is a high priority, and I need to keep on top of it. Can you be ready to leave by seven-thirty tomorrow morning?"

"Sure."

"Good. I'll pick you up at the farm."

* * *

Later that morning Erin parked the car in the garage and walked to the house. She could see Gram waiting for her on the rear porch.

"For heavens sakes, what is going on? When that Gilbert fellow from the FBI called, he insisted he speak to you right away."

Erin climbed the steps and ushered her grandmother back into the kitchen.

"It seems information I gave him yesterday confirms something in their investigation. He wants me in Des Moines tomorrow and hopes I can identify a possible suspect. Sheriff Thomas said he would drive me there."

"Oh, Erin, I'm sorry that you are in the middle of all this! It could spoil your whole vacation. It makes me worry about you."

Erin could see from the look on her grandmother's face that she was very troubled by Erin's growing involvement in the Lawrence killing. "It's fine, Gram. With my work at the firm, procedures like this are routine." Erin knew it was not "routine" to be a witness in a murder case, but she didn't want her grandmother to worry.

"Well, if you say so. It's just too much, this thing with killing and all."

* * *

That evening after supper Erin volunteered to feed Rolf.

Hoping she had convinced Gram that everything was fine, she drove over to the Lawrence farm. Its closed gate had a NO TRESPASSING notice nailed to the top rail. Stepping out she opened the gate then continued down through the grove. Before long, Rolf emerged from the trees and followed alongside. The sound of his barking appeared more friendly than threatening. She assumed he was becoming familiar with the Taylor's car.

After the shepherd had finished his meal, he joined her as she strolled around the property. He would run ahead and then back to her again, happy to have some company.

There were NO TRESPASSING warnings posted on both front and back entrances to the house. After their walk, Erin put the lively dog in for the night.

Before leaving, she gazed at the white frame house. She wondered what it could tell her about the strange man who would never live there again.

* * *

11

Wednesday morning, the bright June sun was already well up in a cloudless sky as Sheriff Thomas in his county patrol unit approached the Taylors' farm. When it stopped near the back porch, Robert stepped out, eager to start on the four hour drive to Des Moines.

Erin was upstairs when she heard his car enter the farmyard.

In the kitchen, Gram was busy stuffing muffins in a paper sack for their trip.

A small kitchen radio had just finished the local farm report from a station in Spencer, Iowa, twenty-eight miles northeast of Parkston. "And here is the KICD seven-thirty weather report. The current temperature is sixty-three degrees at the start of another sunny day. The high will be a pleasant seventy-eight. However, by noon, a quickly moving front from the northwest will bring heavy showers and possible thunderstorms that could contain some hail. Now, a word from Benson's five and dime..."

Florence Taylor heard a knock at the door and turned down the radio's volume. "Come on in, Sheriff!" she called, seeing him on the porch through her kitchen window. "Please, sit down," she said, as he entered. "Erin will be down shortly. Can I pour you a cup of coffee? Maybe some breakfast?"

"No, thanks, Mrs. Taylor," he said, taking a seat at the table. "I'm fine. Had my usual coffee and toast just before I left home."

"I swear, you young people don't eat enough to keep a canary alive," she said.

The sheriff didn't comment. but nodded.

Just then Erin breezed into the kitchen wearing an attractive dress that buttoned down the front. A light summer sweater covered her shoulders. Her only makeup was a touch of lipstick.

"Well, don't we look pretty this morning," Gram said as Erin stood by the table with her purse and a paperback novel she had purchased in Parkston.

"Thanks Gram," she responded.

"Good morning, Sheriff. I'm ready if you are," Erin said. She knew they had a long drive ahead.

When Robert rose from the table, it pleased Erin to see how handsome he looked. He was wearing a white dress shirt, a conservative paisley tie, nicely fitting gray shadow plaid suit pants and black wing-tipped shoes. The only clothes she had seen him in until now were the official khakis, straw hat, and boots.

Erin gave her grandmother a quick hug good-bye and took the sack of muffins without a word of protest.

* * *

There were no speed limits beyond the small towns, and the sheriff wasted little time moving his cruiser south on US 59. In a short while, they were just north of Cherokee when he turned east on state Rt. 3 facing the morning's glare. Erin lowered her visor. She had forgotten to bring her sun glasses.

For a time, there was little conversation between them, so Erin read.

As they traveled further east, the sheriff's short-wave radio crackled with static signaling they were moving out of range, and he turned it off.

"I heard something about bad weather on Gram's radio. Do you think we'll have any problem with it?" she asked, trying to make conversation.

"Not on our way over," he answered, keeping his attention focused on his driving. "We're traveling away from the storm so it shouldn't reach the Des Moines area until later this afternoon."

The sheriff seemed preoccupied with his own thoughts, so she went back to her novel. Now and then, she would look up from her reading to study him. She wondered what occupied his mind. He seemed removed, and his quiet manner did not reveal much. She was aware that people in this rural area were cautious with strangers and wondered how he viewed her. Was she just another outsider from the city?

Later, tired of reading, she looked out the window. Endless green fields separated small towns that spilled by, each looking much like the one before.

Finally, she broke their silence, "Tell me, Sheriff. Has Parkston always been your home?" She already knew the answer from reading about him in Gram's newspaper, and was just making small talk, but their long drive was tiresome with so much time passing in silence.

"Yes, it has," was all he said.

"Where you in the service?"

"After college I joined the army."

"Where did you go to school?"

"University of Iowa in Iowa City." His tone was pleasant, but his responses didn't lead to further conversation. Finally, he asked about her. "I understand you're a lawyer. University of Michigan, wasn't it?"

"Yes," she answered, rather surprised.

"You must have been a good student, graduating at the top of your class."

She started to tell him that she was second in her class and then thought better of it. Erin realized the sheriff had most likely heard her grandfather's version.

Now that he seemed open to talking, she wanted to keep the conversation going. When he revealed that his major had been political science with a minor in criminology, she was impressed. As the time passed, he became more responsive until she questioned him about his part in the war. At that point he simply changed the subject to something else and before long was silent again.

* * *

When they entered the FBI resident agency in Des Moines, it was almost noon. Sheriff Thomas, now wearing a jacket matching his suit pants, gave their names to the receptionist. On the wall behind her desk was a large, bronze circular plaque with the words "Federal Bureau of Investigation" inscribed around the bureau's symbol.

It wasn't long before the reception phone rang with news that agent Gilbert would be right with them. Erin had just picked up a magazine when Gilbert pushed through a pair of heavy glass doors and greeted them.

"Thanks for coming in on such short notice," he said warmly, shaking hands with each of them. "Please follow me to a conference room where we can talk." The agent nodded to the receptionist, and the glass doors made a buzzing noise followed by a click. Gilbert pulled one of the doors and held it open for them.

At first, the locked doors surprised Erin, but she realized this agency was responsible for the nation's internal security. As they entered the conference room, Erin could see it was modern and nicely furnished. The table was long and slightly wider in the middle. Both men stood, waiting for Erin to take one of the chairs.

Almost at once, a young man in a white tunic entered, pushing a food cart. There were sandwiches, soft drinks, coffee and even a plate of cookies. Erin remembered the sack of muffins still in the backseat of the patrol car.

"Being close to lunch time, I thought you two might be hungry, so I ordered some food and drinks," Gilbert said. "Just help yourself. We can eat while we talk. By the way, Miss Hays, I'd like to have our conversations on the record so a stenographer will be joining us in a moment. I'm sure that with your work as an attorney you should be comfortable with that."

"It's fine," she responded, thinking she was the one usually asking the questions."

At that moment, a stenographer entered and quietly sat at the table's far end with her small recorder.

"Good," Gilbert said. "Let's start at the point of your first contact with the suspect and take it through to our meeting on the train in Fort Dodge."

Erin related the newsstand incident when the big man had bumped her and how later she had seen him with a second man in the dining car.

"Did you get a good look at his dinner companion, the one in a brown suit?" Gilbert asked.

"No, when I first came into the car I didn't notice him. He might have been alone at the time. The big man must have arrived some time later, although I never recognized him until couples down the row left their tables. It was the first time I had a clear view. They appeared to be having an argument, although I couldn't hear their conversation. At one point, the man with his back to me stood up, threw down his napkin, then hurried into the aisle heading toward the sleeping car. When he turned to leave the table, I noticed he was wearing glasses. I never saw enough of his face to identify him."

"Did you ever see him at his farm next to your grandparents?"

"No, he wasn't living there the last time I visited. It was more than seven years ago."

"Let's talk about the suspect. Please give a description of him for the record."

"He was a large, muscular man with short blond hair. A light scar below his left eye extending a couple of inches down to his cheek. He was tall. I would say six-one-or-two."

"When did the man with a scar leave?"

"Shortly after the first one."

"Did you ever see either of them again?"

"Not until I remembered being awakened during that night on the train. That's when I called you."

"I hope this is helpful. I realize it's rather sketchy," Erin added.

"No need to apologize, Miss Hays. Your information fits in several ways. The murdered man was wearing the type of clothing you described and glasses. His dinner companion vanished from the train, most likely during the night at Waterloo, Iowa. At that stop, they separate the train. Some of the freight cars are shuttled to a sidetrack for movement north to Minneapolis. When they reconnected the dining and sleeper cars, it would have possibly caused a jolt that awakened you. What we need now is for you to identify the suspect."

"How can I help?"

"Knowing he has an accent, it's possible that your man is either a war refugee or an escaped military prisoner. If so, there could be a record of him. The bureau did a profile search and sent a courier with police photos that fit your description. I would like to get you started on them right away, but please, both of you continue with your lunch."

He thanked the stenographer, and she left as quietly as she had entered.

Erin was finishing a sandwich when a young man wheeled in a cart piled with binders containing hundreds of photographs. It was the first indication of how much work was ahead.

* * *

While the afternoon dragged on, Agent Gilbert was in and out taking messages and checking on her progress. Robert Thomas sat quietly by as Erin slowly turned page after page of photos.

As she leafed through the myriad of mug shots, he studied her. There was that same appraising look in his eyes as that day on the highway, but Erin, her attention focused on the endless catalog of pictures, never noticed.

Later, the sheriff excused himself and left the room to call his office. He wanted Sara to know the interview was taking longer than expected. When he asked about the weather, she related a storm had passed through the county with heavy rain and some hail. There were a few tree limbs down but no serious damage or personal injuries were reported.

* * *

It was nearly five when Gilbert returned to the conference room. Erin, weary from studying hundreds of photos, finally found the man she was looking for. "Here he is! No mistake!" Her voice was a mixture of excitement and relief. Under a front and side view of the Chicago Police Department photo was the name: "Gus Mann, CPD-4739."

"Are you sure this is the man you saw in the station and on the train?" Gilbert asked.

"Yes!" she responded. "Look, you can even see the light scar on his left side profile."

"Great work, Miss Hays! Now we need to check on this Gus Mann. Excuse me while I send a teletype to Chicago. Just relax for a while. I won't be long."

After he left the room, Sheriff Thomas looked at Erin. "It's been a long day, and it may be longer before it's over," he said, standing to stretch after the long hours of sitting.

"What do you mean?" Erin asked, sounding a little weary from looking at so many photos.

"When I called Sara, the storm had passed through the county earlier this afternoon. It's headed this way with heavy rains. We'll be driving directly into it returning to Parkston this evening."

Erin appeared concerned at his news but didn't comment.

Agent Gilbert returned to say because of the late hour they would not have any information on their suspect until after seven the next morning. "A severe storm warning has been issued for the Des Moines area. I suggest it would be best if the two of you stayed in town tonight. There's a fine hotel only a few blocks from here."

"I didn't bring anything for an overnight stay," Erin said at the thought of not returning home.

"I'm sorry for the inconvenience; however, we can provide you both with kits of toiletry items, and the agency will cover your rooms and meal expenses. It is a first-class hotel and has one of the better restaurants in Des Moines," he said, hoping to make the unexpected stay sound more appealing.

Sheriff Thomas looked at Erin. "It seems the only sensible alternative. What do you think?"

She looked at him for a moment, then shrugged. "If the FBI is willing to spring for a good dinner and put me up in a nice hotel, it sure sounds better than driving through a storm in the dark," she said.

"Good!" said Gilbert. "I hoped you would stay. My secretary called and the hotel is holding two rooms, so we're all set."

The agent walked them to the lobby and suggested he would meet them in the hotel grill for breakfast at eight the next morning.

On the street they were greeted by a sky filled with rolling black clouds.

* * *

12

As Erin and Sheriff Thomas drove the few blocks to the hotel, they were happy to find there was an attached parking garage. It was beginning to pour. "The sky is darker than the inside of a coal miner's hat," Thomas remarked, and Erin burst into laughter. It was an unexpected release after the tiresome day she'd spent searching hundreds of photos for Gus Mann.

In the lobby, a polite desk clerk greeted them. He said they were pre-registered for two adjoining rooms on the fifth floor.

Erin glanced at the sheriff when the clerk mentioned the word "adjoining."

He showed no reaction.

Easy girl, this isn't some rendezvous with a stranger, she reminded herself.

The desk clerk continued, "For any of your hotel expenses, just sign the charges to your rooms. Have a good evening, and let us know if you need anything."

On the elevator, Thomas turned to Erin. "With the weather and Gilbert's recommendation for the restaurant, it may be best that we eat here tonight."

"That's fine," she answered.

On the fifth floor, the heavy carpeting muted their footsteps as they approached their adjoining rooms. Erin was holding a key for the first one and used it to open the door.

"I'll call down for a reservation. How does seven o'clock sound?" he asked.

"Okay, I just need time to freshen up and let my grandparents know we won't be back until tomorrow."

"Good. Take your time. I'll meet you in the lobby," he said, moving to the door of his own room.

As Erin entered her room, it was dark. She groped for a wall switch. From the window, a flash of lightning filled the room for a second then it was dark again. During the instant brightness, she found the switch that turned on a floor lamp.

When Erin called the farm, Gram sounded relieved to hear from her and pleased they were staying the night rather than driving back. Gram said they were fine, but it had been a bad storm.

* * *

As the elevator doors opened to the lobby, Erin spotted Sheriff Thomas sitting contently in a wingback chair. He was reading the local newspaper. Noticing her, he laid his paper aside and rose. The movement of her youthful figure and the sight of soft auburn hair falling casually around her shoulders held him, and for a second something inside him stirred then faded as she spoke...

"I'm famished. Do we have a reservation?"

"Yes, but I doubt if we need one. The lobby has been very quiet."

They entered the restaurant and the atmosphere changed. Low lighting replaced the rather harsh brightness of the lobby. A large chandelier glowed softly from the center of the room.

The maitre d', dressed in evening clothes, greeted them with a French flair. "Good evening. May I help you?" His tone was pleasant, although his accent hinted more of something acquired from watching movies than being a native of France.

"We have a reservation in the name of Thomas," the sheriff replied.

"Ah, yes, for two at seven. Please follow me," he said, tucking two menus the size of Rand McNally road maps under his arm.

After they were seated, Erin noticed a string trio softly playing in the far corner.

They each ordered a cocktail. When their drinks came, Sheriff Thomas raised his glass. "Well, Miss Hays, here's to a good day's work! It looks like you found your man."

Erin raised her drink. "To fighting crime," she said, smiling. They touched glasses and laughed. "And please, stop with the Miss Hays! From now on I only answer to Erin. If I keep calling you *sheriff*, the waiter may think I might be someone of less than sterling character. "

"I doubt that very much. However, Erin and Robert it is," he said, smiling at her. For the first time, she was seeing a less reserved side to the person across the table.

They were on their second cocktail when the waiter left with their dinner orders. Erin was feeling pleased at the day's success and excited at spending the night in Des Moines. She was enjoying the evening with Robert. His straightforwardness was different from most of the men in her professional world.

Quiet rhythms from the trio complemented their evening as the two of them talked through dinner. Robert was more open and relaxed.

Maybe a couple of drinks is just what the doctor ordered, she thought. Erin found his conversation interesting and enjoyed the way he made her laugh.

When the waiter had cleared the table except for their coffee, Robert surprised her by asking, "Would the lady attorney care to dance?"

What surprised her even more was how quickly she answered with a simple, "Yes."

Erin and Robert danced on the small floor through a set of three musical numbers. They moved well together. At times the nearness of other dancers required him to pull her close to avoid a collision. She did not resist, enjoying the touch of his masculine body as they danced. When the trio stopped for a break, Erin suppressed a yawn as they returned to their table.

Robert signaled for the check.

* * *

On the fifth floor, they stopped at her room. Robert thanked her for a delightful evening.

"I guess we should thank the FBI," she answered smiling at him.

When Erin turned her key to open the door, she paused for a moment. Despite feeling the weight of a long day, she didn't want their evening to end. During her hesitation, she gazed into his soft gray eyes. Before she could say a word, he quickly kissed her on the cheek, said good night and disappeared into his room.

When Erin entered hers and clicked on the light, she could see a housekeeper had turned down the bed. In a small closet she hung her clothes carefully for the next day and moved naked into the bathroom. She was pleased to find a complimentary terrycloth robe. She quickly washed her face and brushed her teeth. Returning to the bedroom, she threw her robe on a chair next to the double bed, turned out the nightstand light, and slipped under the cool sheets.

The storm had passed and moonlight was streaming in through partially open drapes. In the quiet, she recalled the evening. It was the best time she had had in ages. There was an excitement when she danced with Robert, the feel of his strong arms and the closeness of their bodies as they glided around the small dance floor. She smiled, falling asleep.

During the night, she dreamed an orchestra played while she and a stranger were dancing. He whirled her out and then back. Then, he held her close and kissed her, gently on the lips. When the music faded, he continued to hold her. She responded, melting to him willingly. Then they were together in her bed.

Erin was caressing her pillow as the telephone rang. Groping for a receiver on the nightstand, she mumbled, "Hello."

"Good morning. Are you awake?" It was Robert.

"Not really. What time is it?"

"It's seven-fifteen. Ted Gilbert called and confirmed he would meet us in the grill for breakfast at eight. Take your time. I'll keep him company until you get there."

* * *

Shortly before eight, Erin entered the bright, bustling hotel grill. Robert and Ted Gilbert were seated at a table talking over coffee. Both men stood as she approached. "Good morning," they said, almost in unison.

"Good morning, gentlemen," Erin responded as she joined them.

"It *is* a good morning," Gilbert offered. "Evidently the storm didn't do much damage. Just a heavy rain. I do think it was good that you two stayed over."

"Yes, it was," Robert answered.

Erin watched his expression and looked for another meaning behind the words. But she could see no sign that he was referring to anything but the storm.

As they ate, Robert asked Gilbert if the agency had turned up anything on the suspect.

"The preliminary report showed he has been working as a strong-arm enforcer for a Chicago mobster named Joseph Santini. Mann has been arrested a few times on minor charges but never prosecuted. This information came from the Chicago police files. Until the bureau is able to run a thorough background search, this is all we have for now. We're still checking on the victim."

"Nothing to tie him to Ed Lawrence?" Erin asked.

"No, not yet, but since there's every reason to think they must have known each other prior to your seeing them together on the train, our agency will keep at it until we find the connection. We wouldn't be this far without your help, Miss Hays."

After breakfast, Erin and Robert said goodbye to agent Gilbert in the hotel lobby.

* * *

Heading north on US 69 for their trip back to O'Brien County, Robert was deep in thought. Erin read and watched out the window. She thought about all that had happened since leaving Detroit. When they did talk, the conversation was friendly, yet neither of them said much about their evening together beyond admitting that they had a good time.

It was after one o'clock when the patrol car pulled into Taylor's farmyard. Erin asked Robert in for something to eat, since they hadn't stopped. He declined, saying he needed to check with his office on storm damage.

Erin thanked him for driving her to Des Moines then said good-bye. Waiting outside, she watched until his car disappeared out of sight past the grove. She wondered when she would see him again.

Turning toward the house, she saw Gram at the porch door. "Welcome back, dear! Glad to see you are home safe. Come in and let me fix you something."

To Erin's surprise, she was hungry.

* * *

13

It was light when Erin opened her sleep-filled eyes. She lazily watched as the morning breeze floated the curtains away from a partially open east window. Stretching, she took a deep breath and yawned. For a time, Erin remained under the warm covers and thought about the last two days she'd spent with someone she knew so little about and wondered if she was becoming attracted to him.

When a faint aroma from the kitchen drifted into her bedroom, she moved quickly out of bed. Erin shivered when her bare feet stepped from the braided rug onto the hardwood floor. Reaching into the closet for a pair of old slippers, she headed for the bathroom. A short time later, still in her pajamas and summer robe, she went downstairs to the kitchen.

"Well, good morning," Gram said, as Erin lowered herself into a chair at the table. "Your toast and juice will be ready in a minute."

"I'm really hungry this morning. How about adding a couple of eggs?" Erin's request prompted a pleased look from Gram as she moved to the fridge for eggs and more bacon

Pouring her granddaughter's first cup of coffee, Florence Taylor again voiced her concern about Erin's involvement in the Lawrence affair. She felt it wasn't right to interrupt her vacation by having to travel all the way to Des Moines. Erin said it wasn't a problem as she had enjoyed the trip. The comment appeared to pacify Gram, at least for the moment, as she turned back to her stove and continued cooking breakfast.

"Here we are," Gram said, placing a platter of fresh eggs, honey cured bacon, juice and toast in front of Erin.

"What is Gramps up to this morning?" Erin asked.

"He went to town with Sonny first thing this morning. Something about a part for one of the tractors. By the way, your grandfather wondered if you would go over to the Lawrence Farm and feed the dog. Both Sven and Hank are busy clearing a drainage pipe that plugged up during yesterday's storm."

Dipping a corner of her toast in the egg yolk, Erin said she would be happy to take care of Rolf.

After breakfast, Erin showered and dressed, tied her hair back and pulled on a clean pair of jeans, tennis shoes, and an old sweatshirt she found back in the closet.

Downstairs, she told Gram good-bye, grabbed their Buick's keys off the hook and headed out the kitchen door.

* * *

Rays of sunlight found their way through the trees and danced on the windshield as she drove down the lane at Lawrence's farm. When Erin stopped and stepped from the car, she could hear Rolf barking in the barn. When she opened the cream separator room door, the shepherd made his now-familiar dash to check his dish. Finding it empty, he ran back barking at her to hurry.

"You're hungry this morning, aren't you, boy!"

Almost as if to answer, he looked at her with his alert brown eyes and barked again. She knew it was past his feeding time because Bert, or one of his men, normally let him out and fed him much earlier.

As she pulled the large sack of dog food down the steps and began pouring its contents into his large bowl, the big dog tried to nuzzle her out-of-the-way causing part of his food to miss its target and spill on the ground. "Hey, take it easy!" she demanded, half smiling with the thought that Gram might enjoy feeding this ravenous guy.

As Rolf eagerly devoured his food, Erin replaced his food sack on the porch. Turning to leave, she noticed a lower window section was missing from the kitchen door. A few jagged pieces were still in the frame. She knew it had not been broken when Gilbert and Robert had entered on Sunday. Cautiously turning the knob, Erin opened the door. When she saw broken glass scattered inside on the floor, it confirmed someone had forced their way in. She wondered if one of Robert's deputies, not having a key, could have broken the window to check on something inside. That notion vanished when she stepped into the kitchen. Drawers were lying on the floor. Their contents were strewn everywhere. An eerie feeling held her as she stared at open cupboard doors with dishes scattered and broken. Stepping carefully so she wouldn't disturb anything, she moved further into the house.

Everywhere the scene was the same. It looked as if a madman had trashed the place. Erin recalled Agent Gilbert's comment about how neat Lawrence kept his home. Then she froze. Standing in the middle of the torn cushions and overturned furniture, she suddenly realized that whoever had done this could still be hiding somewhere in the house. Holding her breath, she listened, straining for any sign that would suggest she was not alone. The house was silent. The only sound was that of her own heavy breathing. "Let's not panic," she whispered, as if someone might hear her.

Quickly she searched for the telephone and found it in the hall. The receiver was still on the hook, and it appeared untouched. Her hand was shaking as she cranked the handle and listened. There was no response. She turned the handle again. "Come on, answer…"

Then a voice came over the line, "Number, please?"

"Please ring the Sheriff's Office. I don't know the number." There was a pause, and then Erin could hear ringing on the other end.

"Sheriff's office." It was Sara the dispatcher.

"Sara, this is Erin Hays, I need to talk with Sheriff Thomas. I'm at the Lawrence farm. Someone has broken in, and the place is a mess."

"He's not here, Miss Hays. Hold on while I try to raise him on the radio."

Erin could hear Sara calling the sheriff, asking him to respond. She repeated her call three times.

"I'm sorry, Miss Hays. He doesn't answer." In the background, Erin could hear the familiar crackling sound of the short-wave. Then she heard his voice.

"This is the sheriff. What is it Sara?"

"Erin Hays is calling for you. She is at the Lawrence place, and someone has broken in."

"I'm on the highway about seven miles south. Tell her I'll be there in just a few minutes."

"Roger. Will do. Dispatch out."

Erin thanked Sara and, still being careful not to disturb anything, quickly left. Once outside, she felt relieved, removed from the possibility of an intruder.

Before Robert's arrival, she thought it would be best to corral Rolf and get him back in the barn. At the porch steps, she could see his bowl was empty, clean as if it had been washed. Even food spilled on the ground was gone.

In the distance, she could hear him barking. As she moved behind the barn, Erin could see Rolf chasing after something far out in the east pasture. Then he disappeared out of sight. "Well so much for that idea," she said.

When Erin returned, Robert's patrol car was speeding down the dirt lane and skidded to a halt near the Taylors' Buick. Robert jumped out and quickly moved toward Erin. "Are you all right?"

"I'm fine, but the house is a mess," Erin said. "I called thinking that you should know as soon as possible." Actually, The thought of an intruder lurking in the house was unsettling, and she wanted him there.

"It's good you called," he said, taking her arm. "Let's see what you found." Together they walked up the porch steps and entered through the still open door. "Was the door closed?" he asked.

"Yes, whoever did this apparently broke out the windowpane and unlocked it from inside."

"Stay close, but be careful not to get your fingerprints on anything."

Erin remembered she used the wall phone but didn't comment. As they entered, she followed Robert as he walked through each room. It appeared someone had gone through everything in the place. Erin wondered what it could be that was so important.

"Well, I don't know what they were after, but they sure made a mess trying." Robert stopped at a door leading down to the basement and suggested he should go down alone. In a minute, he was back reporting it had also been ransacked.

"We'd better go back outside. I'll call Gilbert and let him know about the break-in." Returning to patrol car, Robert radioed Sara asking which deputy was closest to the Lawrence Farm.

She answered that Deputy Martin had just returned from patrol.

"Have Frank join me here right away. As soon as he arrives, I'll return to the office."

In a short time, Deputy Martin's cruiser came into the farmyard and quickly pulled up next to the sheriff's car.

Robert said he wanted Erin away from the Lawrence place. "I suggest you go back to the Taylors'. Whoever did this could still be in the area and might come back if they didn't find what they wanted."

She offered no resistance to his concern and headed for the Buick.

Sheriff Thomas and his deputy watched as Erin's car traveled out of sight past the grove.

Robert gave his deputy instructions not to let anyone on the property.

"Stay outside and keep your radio on. Carry your shotgun and call in to Sara every half hour. I'll be in my office. Any questions?"

"Got it, boss. Will do." The young deputy moved with eager determination to his patrol car for the twelve gauge weapon.

When Sheriff Thomas drove past Taylor's farm on his way to town, he could see their Buick parked in the garage.

* * *

14

Bert Taylor was in his office writing out the weekly paychecks for his three farmhands. When Erin entered, he looked up and smiled. "Were you able to feed the dog?"

"Yes," she answered. Erin was silent for a time, reluctant to mention the break-in. Yet she knew it would most likely be all over town before the day was over. "There's some more bad news over at the Lawrence place."

"What now?" he asked.

"Someone broke in and ransacked the house. I called Sheriff Thomas, and he has a deputy guarding the property."

"I can't believe it!" Bert responded. "Ed being killed was bad enough. Can this thing get any worse?" As he spoke, there was obvious misgiving in his voice. "Lawrence was odd, but I just thought that being from a foreign country made him seem different."

"Whatever he was doing involved something he couldn't control." Then Erin added her concern about telling Gram. "She has been upset, and I'm sure this news won't help."

"Don't worry about your grandmother. She's a tough old girl. Florence gets emotional, but truth be told, in the long run she deals with most things better than I do. You might as well tell her what happened because she'll hear about it soon enough anyway. This is big news around here. Folks will be hashing over this Lawrence thing all summer."

Her grandfather was right. At the noon meal Sonny, Sven, and Hank took turns, between extra helpings, speculating about what was behind the break-in. It surprised Erin when Gram didn't say much, but the look on her face showed she was growing even more unhappy with the whole affair.

While Erin helped with the dishes, Gram was fussing again. "It's too bad your time here has to be spoiled by this awful mess. I hope it's cleared up soon. Then we can all breathe a little easier."

Erin would never tell her grandmother she found the mystery surrounding the Lawrence farm exciting and a welcome diversion from her job in Detroit.

* * *

Later, that afternoon, Erin promised to stop at the grocery for Gram. When she entered the garage office, her grandfather was busy punching keys on an ancient adding machine. "Hi, Gramps," Erin said, as she lowered herself in a chair by his desk.

As he looked up and saw her, his blue eyes twinkled. Hi, there," he said. "Just adding up some bills. What are you up to?"

"I thought about taking the car into town and putting some gas in it. I seem to be the only one using it."

"Don't be spending your money. Stop at the Skelly Station. They give me a rebate if I buy enough each month. Just have them charge the gas to my account. By the way, you could do me a favor while you're there if you would mail these letters. Our mailman has already been here, and I'd like them to go out today."

"No problem. Gram asked me to pick up some items from the grocery store. I'm happy to do something. I use your car so often."

* * *

It was mid-afternoon when Erin pulled into a parking space in front of a small brick building that was the Parkston Post Office. Inside, she pushed her grandfather's mail through a brass slot marked "Letters" and moved to the counter to buy a few stamps.

Back in her car, Erin drove down the east side of the square past the old hotel and Sheriff's Office. A block later she pulled into the Skelly Station and stopped next to a tall gas pump marked "Ethyl."

A young man wearing a Chicago Cubs ball cap came out of the station's single work bay, wiped his hands on a rag and stopped at her driver side window. He had a streak of grease on his cheek and another on the end of his nose. "Good afternoon. Are you Miss Hays?" he asked in a friendly voice.

"Yes."

"Mr. Taylor called. Besides gas, he wanted me to be sure and check the oil."

"That's fine," Erin responded, turning her attention to the patrol car that had just pulled in and stopped across the pump-island.

Robert emerged from his cruiser and addressed the young man. "Please fill it up with premium and check the tire pressure when you are finished with Miss Hays."

"Sure thing, Sheriff," the attendant answered.

Erin was still sitting in the car when Robert stepped over the island and stopped by her window. He bent down until their eyes met.

"Hi," he said. His voice was decidedly pleasant.

"Hi," she answered back, glad to see him again.

"Would you stop by my office for a few minutes before leaving town?"

"Sure, I have an errand to do for Gram first. Then I'll come by." She wondered if he had talked with Ted Gilbert.

* * *

A half hour later, she was at Robert's office door. He was seated behind his desk reading and stood up as she entered. He asked her to come in and close the door. He seemed concerned.

"What did you want?" she asked, taking a seat across from him.

"I thought you would like to know that Gilbert is having the State Police Investigation Unit out of Sioux City go over everything at the Lawrence house. He wants them to dust for fingerprints and inspect for anything that might identify the intruder. He asked to have my deputies keep a watch each night until their inspection is completed."

"Will that be a problem?" she asked, wondering why he had wanted the door closed to tell her something she was sure his staff must know.

"Not really. I called in my deputy who has been on vacation. It was lucky he was just working around the house and not away somewhere.

Once the state police team has completed their investigation, they will seal the place and that should be it."

He seemed to be rambling. It was not like him.

"When will they be arriving?" Erin asked.

"First thing in the morning. Their team is based in Sioux City. It's just a little over an hour from the farm."

Erin noticed he was repeating himself.

"I need to ask you a favor."

"Sure, if I can. What is it?"

He seemed to be avoiding her gaze. "Would you ask Bert if he could keep Lawrence's dog in the barn while the police are there?"

"I'm sure he will."

"There's one more thing."

"Yes?" she said, waiting.

"Would you have dinner with me Saturday night?"

Surprised at the request, she didn't answer right away. "What did you have in mind?" she asked.

"There is a place just north of here…a restaurant…actually more of a road house. It's quite popular."

"Would I have to dress up for this event?"

"No, you can wear what you like."

Erin realized that she still had not given him her answer. When Erin she would be happy to go, he looked relieved, as if just informed that surgery would not be necessary.

"What time?" she asked.

"How about seven? I can pick you up at the Taylors'."

"That sounds fine." Erin answered.

Robert smiled for the first time since her arrival.

*   *   *

On the drive back to the farm, Erin thought about the way he had acted. The normally assured and confident war hero who had faced enemy fire to save his men had acted like a high school freshman asking for his first date. She understood why he had wanted the office door closed.

Erin parked in the garage and started for the house when she saw her grandfather walking up from the fields. "Hi, Gramps!" she called," I need to check with you on something."

"What is it?" he asked, catching up with her at the porch steps. His shoes were heavy with mud.

"Tomorrow morning the state police will be at the Lawrence place. Robert asked if you would secure Rolf in the barn until they're through with their investigation."

Removing his cap, he paused to catch a breath. Erin could see small beads of sweat on his forehead. "That's fine. I'll have one of the men make sure he's fed and back in the barn."

"Thanks, Gramps. I'll call Robert and let him know."

At supper that evening Erin's grandmother voiced concern about Erin's need for some social life during her visit.

Bert chimed in, "Now, Florence, Erin is a grown woman. Let her decide what she wants to do."

"I'm just trying to be sure she enjoys her time here. Erin, we could have one of your friends from earlier visits over for dinner, maybe Saturday night. I could fix something special."

"That's sweet of you, Gram, but I'm planning to have dinner with Robert tomorrow night."

"Robert?" Gram asked with a puzzled look.

"Robert Thomas. You know, the sheriff."

"Well, my goodness!" Gram responded, amazed at her granddaughter's news. "Good for you! He's the most eligible bachelor in the county. It's high time he found someone to spend time with."

"Whoa there, Gram! This is just two people having dinner together. I really am surprised he asked me anyway."

"It's no surprise if you ask me," Bert cut in, reaching for seconds. "The local war hero asks the prettiest girl in the county out on a date. Sounds like a real match for sure."

"I think it's just great!" Gram added, beaming her approval.

"Let's not get ahead of ourselves, you two. I'll be going back to Michigan soon." Attempting to steer the conversation to another subject, Erin asked about something she knew was on her grandfather's mind. "Gramps, what will you do now about leasing that Lawrence property?"

"I don't know. I'm planning to meet with Joe Butler in the morning to see if anything can still be worked out." His tone sounded less than optimistic.

"You could have a problem," Erin commented. "The farm could be tied up in escrow for some time. It depends on whether Lawrence has a will and what it stipulates. Do you know about his relatives?"

"Not sure," Bert answered. "I think he has someone in Chicago, but he never really mentioned any family. Florence heard, from her cousin at the bank, that Lawrence listed a man's name on some of the paperwork they have on file." He looked at his granddaughter. "Would you like to go with me in the morning? You might enjoy meeting Joe. He's a nice old gentleman. The two of you could exchange some lawyer talk."

Both women stared at him across the table, and then laughed at his "lawyer talk."

* * *

Later the next morning, Erin was with her grandfather in the Ford pickup on their way to town. In Parkston, he parked in front of a one story gray stone building that was Joe Butler's law office. A wide picture window facing the street displayed his name in bold, gilded letters bordered in black: "JOSEPH BUTLER, ATTORNEY-AT-LAW." Bert and Erin walked up four steps to the front door and entered a reception area.

A woman Erin guessed to be in her mid to late fifties, looked up at them from her typewriter. "Good morning, Bert. Nice to see you. And this must be your granddaughter, Miss Hays."

At this point in her visit, Erin would have been surprised if someone in Parkston had not known who she was.

"Erin, this is Bertha. She's Joe's right hand. She's worked for him so long that sometimes it seems like he's working for her."

The woman grinned at the remark. "That would be the day."

"It's a pleasure to meet you, Bertha," Erin said with a polite smile.

"Nice to meet you also, Miss Hays. Please go on in. Joe is expecting you."

Bert said, "Thanks," and headed down a hallway with Erin close behind. They passed an open door to a conference room which contained a heavy looking table surrounded by six wooden arm chairs. She followed her grandfather as he walked next door into Joe Butler's office. As they entered, the old man was bent over an ancient desk. He was busy writing on a long yellow pad.

"Good morning, Joe," Bert said, raising the level of his voice.

The elderly man looked up, startled at their presence. His gray, thinning hair exposed the pale skin on his head.

Erin noticed his blue suit jacket hung loosely from his large frame.

"Well, good morning, Bert! Sorry I didn't hear you come in. My darn hearing aid is on the fritz again." He moved with effort, slowly rising to greet them and extended a frail hand to Bert. Then, he turned to Erin. "This pretty lady must be your granddaughter."

"Nice to meet you," Erin responded. She shook the elderly man's hand.

"Yes, I remember your grandfather telling me about their bright granddaughter with the firm in Detroit." He paused. "Please sit down. Would either of you like some coffee? I could use another cup myself."

Bert said he would like some, black. Erin passed on his offer.

She watched as the aging attorney, slightly bent, moved in short measured steps out of his office and turned down the hall. While he was gone, Erin looked around the room. Wood filing cabinets stacked with folders lined a far wall. Built-in shelves on the opposite side of the office held a mass of books, some looking very old. Behind the large desk next to a window were diplomas and certificates, along with a framed photo of men in army uniforms from another era. The room was a history of the old man's life. She was impressed that, while the place showed its age, everything was exceptionally clean.

"Here we are," he said, returning with two huge ivory colored mugs of steaming coffee. He set one in front of Bert. "I guess you want to talk about the lease," he said, slowly easing into his high back chair.

Sipping carefully on the hot drink, Bert confirmed with a nod, as Joe continued.

"To the best of my knowledge, Lawrence left no will. Anyway, his property will go through probate until we can locate some heirs. If not, the circuit court judge will have to make a ruling. Meanwhile, I am afraid there is nothing we can do. It's a shame, but for now his land will just stay as it is."

"What if there are no legitimate heirs?" asked Bert.

"Then the property will most likely go to the county and would be sold at a sheriff's auction unless the state has some claim. I'm sorry."

Bert sat quietly for a time, then let out a long sigh. "It really isn't any financial loss. I didn't buy any seed for planting or make other preparations. The only thing is your fee for drawing up the lease."

"Just forget it, Bert," Joe said. "You have given me so much business over the years, I wouldn't feel right taking anything. Let's just call the whole thing even."

Joe turned to Erin. "Tell me, young lady, how do you like practicing in a large firm like Davis, Clark, Adams and Hays?"

Erin was amazed how he so effortlessly recited the name of her firm.

He saw the surprise on her face and explained. "I met your dad some years back when he and his brother Maxwell passed through Parkston on a trip to South Dakota. Maxwell was looking into something for your father's firm. It was about a company in Sioux Falls if I remember rightly. On the way, they stopped to visit with Bert and Florence. We all had dinner together and exchanged business cards. I fished it out when Bert said you were coming in with him."

Erin was impressed Joe still remembered the meeting with her dad and uncle from so long ago.

Bert took a last drink of his coffee and looked at the old attorney. "Well, Joe, I need to get back to the farm. As a way of thanks for you efforts, why don't you come out for Sunday dinner? We'd be glad to have your company."

"I would like that," Joe answered. "Since my wife passed on, I eat too many meals at the café here in town. Everyone knows what a great cook Florence is. You can count on my coming, Just give me a call and tell me when to be there."

* * *

15

Later that afternoon Erin was upstairs preparing for her evening with Robert. It was the only real date with a man in months, and she found the prospect of another dinner with him exciting.

After her shower, Erin was in the bedroom looking over her limited selection of travel clothing. Remembering Robert had said the restaurant would be casual, she decided to wear her new beige linen slacks and a white sleeveless blouse with wide collars and a deep v-shaped neckline revealing just a hint of her breasts. Slipping on the low-heeled pumps she had worn on the train, Erin looked at herself in a full-length mirror on the bedroom door. *Well, this should keep his attention,* she thought, satisfied the outfit complemented her appearance. In the bathroom, she applied lipstick, made a brisk descent down to the kitchen where her grandparents were finishing their Saturday night supper.

"Boy, some heads will turn tonight!" Bert Taylor exclaimed.

"Why, thank you, Sir," Erin responded, moving into a chair at their table.

Through the open window, they could hear the sound of car tires crunching on the farmyard gravel. Erin glanced at the wall clock. It was almost seven.

"Sounds like your escort has arrived," Bert said, giving his wife an impish wink.

When Robert knocked at the screen door, Bert called, "Come on in!"

As the sheriff entered, Erin saw how nice he looked for their evening together. His long-sleeved, casual shirt complemented the tan pleated slacks and a pair of loafers which had become so popular since the war. She nodded her approval, then saying she would be just be a minute, she disappeared into the hall.

"Please sit down and have something," Gram said.

Before he could decline the offer, Erin returned. She wore her only summer sweater draped loosely over her shoulders. "I'm ready." She beamed at Robert and blew kiss good-bye to her grandparents.

As they left the house, it surprised Erin to see a dark blue, two-door Oldsmobile in place of the familiar county patrol unit.

"My, what a nice-looking car!" she commented as he held the door for her. The leather seats gave the interior that "new car" smell. "It looks like it just came from the dealer," she said.

"Thanks. I bought it over a year ago," he said, entering the driver's side. "I don't use it much. Most of the time I'm driving the county cruiser while this one is in the garage at home." Robert was quiet as they headed down the county road, reflecting his usual reserved nature. When they reached the highway, he broke his silence by telling Erin how nice she looked.

Erin thanked him, pleased by his compliment. "What did the state police turn up at the farm?" she asked.

"I was there a good part of the day," he said. "Nothing turned up showing who was in the house or what they were looking for. The investigating team dusted for fingerprints and held some items for their lab in Des Moines. What the intruder was looking for is still a mystery."

Erin wondered if the answer might still be hidden somewhere in the house.

* * *

Seven miles north of Parkston, near the town of Sanborn, Robert turned into the parking area of their destination. It was a long, low building with rough hewn wood siding. Erin could see a huge sign, in dark red letters on the roof: "TOM'S STEAK HOUSE." Smoke from somewhere behind the restaurant curled up over the sign filling the air with the scent of something cooking on a grill.

"This may look a little rough on the outside, but the food is good,"

Robert said, seeming to apologize for his taking her there for their first date.

As they climbed up large plank steps, Erin thought the place was quaint.

Behind a small stand inside the entrance, a man with a shaggy mustache, wearing a western style shirt complete with string tie, looked up from his reservation book. He extended his hand. "Sheriff Thomas. Welcome!" Tom Henderson, the owner, said. "It's been a long time since your last visit! I'm glad you called because it's been a busy Saturday night. I've saved a corner table in the second room for you and your charming companion."

He smiled at Erin, picked up two menus, asked them to follow him and headed through the first dining area. It was large with a long bar across the front. Heavy timbers supported the ceiling and weathered barn wood covered the walls. Hunting and fishing regalia hung at random, scattered among brightly colored neon signs advertising various brands of beer. The place was busy, every table filled.

As they followed their host, many customers recognized Robert. Some called out greetings to the popular sheriff. There were several glances at the attractive stranger by his side. When they passed though an archway into the second room, the owner stopped at the only unoccupied table.

"Here we are," their host said, pulling back a chair for Erin.

After they sat down, a waitress stopped by and took their drink orders.

Across the table, Robert appeared pleased. "Thanks for accepting my dinner invitation," he said. "I enjoyed our night in Des Moines. I must confess, it has been a while since I spent an evening with a woman."

His comment surprised Erin. It was the first time he had ever mentioned his social life. She found it hard to believe he didn't have someone special. Robert seemed so popular and well-liked. Erin knew her social life wasn't exactly bubbling over either.

"I had a good time also," she confided.

When their drinks arrived, Robert raised his glass. "To the prettiest woman in O'Brien County."

"Oh, just the county? I was hoping for wider coverage." Then Erin laughed as she touched his glass, and they took the first taste of their cocktails.

When the waitress came, they both ordered steaks and beer. Erin made a remark about having to go on a diet when she returned to Detroit. "I'm happy I could still get into my clothes this evening."

Robert was well aware of how slim she was and knew better than to go anywhere near the topic of a woman's weight. He changed the subject.

"How long do you plan to stay with your grandparents?" he asked.

"It's rather open for now. My firm doesn't expect me back for a while. Another week or so."

Robert was pleased they could have the chance for more time together. After awhile, as they sipped their drinks, he seemed at a loss for conversation and was quiet again thinking about the first time they met on the highway and their trip to Des Moines.

"Hello there? Sheriff?" she said, seeing his faraway look.

"Sorry." He flushed a little at the thought of ignoring her.

The waitress saved the moment, by returning with their dinners. "Here we are," she said, placing the gigantic steaks and two beers on their table.

"It looks wonderful," Erin commented, looking down at a thick juicy T-bone still sizzling on an oval platter.

"Yes, they do look good," he agreed. He waited for her to take the first bite.

For a time, they were quiet, busy eating.

Then, Erin broke the silence, "I just can't stop thinking of why someone was so intent on tearing apart the Lawrence place. What could they be after?"

"Well, whatever it was, they sure went through everything in the house. The lead investigator said there was hardly anything left untouched. Whoever did it even pulled up the rugs looking for a possible hiding place in the flooring."

"This whole incident with Lawrence's murder and the disturbance in his home keeps nagging at me. There has to be a connection," Erin said.

"Well, whatever they were looking for must be important if they were willing to kill for it," Robert said. "I have a strong concern about your going over there alone to feed the dog. Why don't you just let one of Bert's men do it?"

"Please, don't worry about me," she said.

Erin had barely finished speaking when they could hear shouts coming from the front room. The noise was loud, rising well above the conversations from surrounding tables. It was obvious someone was upset and confrontational.

Before long, their host appeared looking distressed. "Sheriff, I'm sorry to interrupt your dinner, but we have a problem. Herb Nelson is in the next room and has had too much to drink. The Farm Bureau agent is at the next table with his wife, and Herb started an argument with him. I tried to calm Herb down, but he wouldn't listen. Would you mind giving me a hand with this?"

Robert stood up and turned to Erin. "I'm sorry. Would you excuse me for a few minutes?"

"Certainly. I'll be fine."

The restaurant owner gave Erin a weak smile and followed Robert into the next room.

Near the bar, two men were facing each other, shouting. Before the sheriff could reach them, the intoxicated man took a wild swing at his opponent. Unsteady on his feet, the drunk fanned the air, missed his target and whirled around, falling into an empty chair at the next table. A woman at the table jumped up, screaming at his untimely arrival. Trying to orient himself, he struggled to stand just as the sheriff closed the distance and placed his hand on the drunken man's shoulder to hold him in the chair.

"Take it easy, Herb, Robert said in a low steady voice. At the same time, he kept enough pressure on the man's shoulder to prevent him from getting up.

"Take your hand off me!" The drunk demanded "I'm going to punch that no-good son-of-a- bitch right back to his do-nothing office."

"Now, Herb, I would hate to see you spend the weekend in the county jail," Robert said. His words were calm, but spoken in a tone of authority. For the first time, the man looked up and realized who was holding him down. He cocked his head and looked at the sheriff and then back to the Farm Bureau Agent still standing at the next table. The agent, a much bigger man, glared back, his fists still clenched, ready for combat. Herb shook his head as if to clear his vision and made a feeble effort to stand. With his hand still on the man's shoulder, the Sheriff asked the agent to sit down. He did without any further comment. His wife, who had been hiding safely behind her husband, slowly returned to her chair.

"How about some fresh air, Herb? I think it will make you feel better," Robert said.

Then he turned to the room and asked everyone to please continue with their dinners while he and Mr. Nelson stepped outside. Helping the now passive drunk onto his wobbly legs, Sheriff Thomas guided him toward the exit. The hum of conversation returned to the dining room.

Outside, the man sat quietly on the front steps of the roadhouse. He looked tired and sad. Robert asked his host, hovering nearby, to keep an eye on Herb while he telephoned a deputy to come by to take the man home.

When Robert returned to Erin at their table, he apologized. "I'm sorry for leaving in the middle of dinner."

"Hey, you were just doing your job. I couldn't hear your conversation, but it seems you managed to settle everything. What was the trouble?"

"Herb has a farm near here. The poor guy is a good man. He lost his only son in the war, then his wife died last year. He's been working the place by himself. The storm that came through when we were in Des Moines hit his place with hail which damaged some of his crops."

"Sounds like the poor man has been through some rough times," Erin said.

"Farming has been tough for many of these people, and they look to the federal government for help. Too often, it's slow coming if it comes at all. Tonight Herb had too much whisky and took out his troubles on the local agricultural agent whose table was near the bar."

As they finished eating, Tom Henderson stopped by. "Sheriff, thanks for your help. A fight is not what I need with a full house on Saturday night. It was fortunate you were here to settle it."

"Don't mention it, Tom. It's just part of the job. Glad I could help."

"Well, thanks again. And, by the way, don't look for a check. The dinner is on me. I'll make sure your waitress gets a proper tip. Now, is there anything else either of you would like?"

"Just coffee would be fine," Erin responded.

"Coffee for me also," Robert said.

Later, when Robert tried to get a check from their waitress, she just smiled and told them to please come again soon. As they said goodnight to their host at the front door, Robert thanked him for the dinner but said there would be no more free meals. They shook hands and Robert and Erin left.

* * *

In the car, Erin told him the next time dinner would be her treat. Robert chuckled, saying he still hadn't paid for hers. He appeared pleased she had mentioned a next time.

As they drove back to Parkston, Erin commented she didn't have any idea of where he lived.

"When I returned from the service, there was an old place that always intrigued me, so with my back pay from the army, I bought it. It's been a real challenge to restore, but I've enjoyed the work."

"It sounds interesting. I'd like to see it some time."

"Well, it's still early. Would you like to stop by for a while?"

Erin looked at the clock on the dashboard. It was a little after nine. "I've been going to bed so early at the farm. It might be nice to stay up for a change," she said.

Robert was pleased. It would give them a chance to spend more time together.

When they reached Parkston, he turned west from the highway down a concrete paved street for six blocks before he slowed. "Here we are."

The property was on a corner lot. Erin could just make out the house in the dusk. It was a two-and-a-half story, wood-framed Victorian. She could see some of the details indicating its styling. High windows in the tower supported a six-sided wood shingled roof.

"Robert, from what I can tell, it looks charming."

He stopped the Oldsmobile in front of a two-car garage.

Eager to see inside his house, Erin jumped out before he could open her door. She followed him on a flagstone path to a screened summer porch.

When they entered the kitchen, he switched on the lights. "Just make yourself at home. There are no hidden secrets in this house, at least none I'm aware of."

"That's good," she answered, smiling at his subtle reference to the Lawrence place. "I'd love to wander around if you don't mind. Your place looks intriguing."

"Before you start, would you like something to drink?"

"What are you having?"

"Another beer, I guess."

"Then make it two," she answered, beginning to look around, impressed with his kitchen. It was bright and modern with all the latest appliances. No sink full of dirty dishes. It was not what she expected from a bachelor.

As he opened the refrigerator to get their drinks, she was already moving into the dining room, searching the wall for a switch. When she found it, the room became bathed with light from a crystal chandelier. Moldings framed the lower third of the painted walls, and a floral printed wallpaper covered the upper portion to the ceiling. There was no furniture. Erin could smell the varnish from the refinished oak floors and reached down to remove her shoes.

Robert rejoined her. He held two glasses of cold beer. "Don't worry about the floor. I finished it some time ago."

She took the drink from his hand. "No problem, I'm more comfortable without shoes anyway."

Robert watched her as she studied the room.

When she lifted the glass and took a small sip; the light from the chandelier caught the brilliance in her eyes.

"Your dining area is very attractive. Did you do all the work?" she asked.

"Most of it. I'll tackle wallpaper, moldings, and painting. I did refinish the floor. When it comes to challenges like plumbing and electrical, I leave those things to the professionals. Would you like to see the rest of the house?"

"Yes, I would," she answered, wondering if the rest of it looked this good. Erin followed him as they went from room to room and marveled at what a great job he had done, most of it himself. All the rooms were furnished except the dining room and one bedroom upstairs that held his tools and decorating supplies.

When Robert showed her the main bedroom, Erin paused to wonder who might have shared his magnificent canopy bed.

Back in the living room, Robert turned on a floor lamp. "Would you like some music?"

"Sure," she said. Erin lowered herself into one end of the sofa and tucked one leg beneath her. She watched as he moved across the room to a floor model Zenith radio.

As the large round dial came to life with a soft glow, a deep professional sounding voice filled the room, "This is station KICD, coming to you live from The Roof Garden Pavilion overlooking beautiful Lake Okoboji. Tonight we are sending you the dance music of Tommy Dorsey and his orchestra."

Moving to the sofa, Robert sat at the other end, slipped off his shoes and faced her.

For the next two hours, they talked. Their evening passed quickly and Erin enjoyed being with him. Their conversation went well until she asked about his former fiancée. He evaded her question and became silent.

Suddenly, a bright flash of lighting flooded the room. The radio responded with a loud burst of static. The lights went out, leaving them in darkness for a moment. Then they came back on again. Robert rose, saying he wanted to see if the phone was still working. He mentioned that after office hours the telephone operator acted as his night dispatcher. She called him if there was a problem. After finding the phone was working, he returned just as the radio announcer interrupted the music to say a summer storm was passing through Dickinson and O'Brien Counties. There was so much static that Robert turned the radio off.

Erin, beginning to look sleepy, asked what time it was.

"Eleven-fifteen. I better get you home before your grandparents wonder where you are."

"If they mention it, I'll tell them you had me in protective custody," Erin said with a giggle. She was feeling the lingering effects of her beer and the late hour.

Robert was still on his feet. He looked down at her. He offered his hand to help her up. As Erin rose from the sofa, she tilted forward, falling against him. For a second, neither of them moved. Then, his arms encircled her waist. He pulled her even closer. She did not resist when he kissed her fully on the lips and she sensed the energy of his body. Wrapping her arms around his neck, she eagerly kissed him back, then quickly she released her embrace and quietly told him it was time to go.

As they hurried into his car, the first drops began to splash down from clouds pierced with lightning.

* * *

Rain was falling when Robert stopped in the Taylor's farmyard near the house.

Erin turned to him, "Don't get out. I'll just make a dash for the porch." In the soft light from the car's instrument panel, she studied the tender look he gave her.

"It was a lovely evening. We should do it again," she whispered. Her words were barely audible over the falling rain as it drummed on the car's surface.

He pulled her to him, kissed her one last time, then said, "We will."

Touching his face with her hand, she said goodnight, opened her car door and ran for the porch. For a brief moment, a flash of lightning filled the farmyard as if it were midday. Then it was gone. When she opened the kitchen door, the inside light framed her silhouette as she waved good-bye.

* * *

16

The next morning when Erin came down for breakfast, Gram was not at her usual place in the kitchen. The house seemed empty without her bustling about. Then Erin remembered it was Sunday, and her grandparents would be in Parkston attending church.

After the steak dinner with Robert, she felt a bowl of cereal with some fruit would be more than enough this morning. The electric coffee percolator next to the stove was on and filled with hot coffee.

Sitting down at the table, she saw a note next to the sugar bowl, written on a pad advertising fertilizer. The writing was in Gramp's condensed style, as if he were sending a ten-cents-a-word telegram:

> *Erin, we have gone to church.*
> *Please take the pickup and feed Rolf.*
> *Love, BT*

Erin smiled when she saw the initials. He always used them as his signature even on his bank checks.

When she finished her breakfast, Erin washed the spoon and bowl and placed them in the sink's dish drainer. After her shower, she dressed and headed for the garage.

* * *

At the entrance to the Lawrence Farm, Erin stopped in front of a closed gate. From behind the wheel, she could see new notices tacked over the original ones Robert's deputies had placed there. Bold letters warned trespassing was a federal offense.

Wet leaves from the previous night's soaking rain glistened in the sunlight as she drove through the grove. When Erin stopped in the farmyard and stepped down from the pickup, she could see there was a warning poster tacked to the kitchen door.

On the porch, Rolf's food was still in the far corner. She decided it was easier to fill his bowl before letting him loose. When she did let him out, he made the usual dash for the porch steps and his breakfast.

Erin watched him for a time then decided to walk around the house. On the front door, there was another no-entry notice. She remembered seeing one posted on the barn.

On the south side of the house, Erin came to a large group of lilac bushes still wet from last night's storm. The weight of water on the leaves bowed the branches enough so that she could observe a slanted metal cover normally hidden from sight. Curious, she pushed aside the wet branches to move closer to inspect her find. There were two handles attached to each side of the iron doors that opened from the middle. *It might be the cover for a rain cistern,* she thought, looking up to the edge of the roof for a downspout. There was none. Still curious, she reached down and pulled on one of the handles. The cover didn't move. She tried again. This time she tugged with both hands. With a creaking of rusty hinges, the right hand cover began to rise. It opened to reveal steps leading down to a door. *Well look at this!* she thought. When Erin opened the left cover, sunlight spilled down the damp, musty steps. There were spider webs stretched from wall to wall. Dirt and mildew covered the door at the bottom. She wondered why the inspection team had not tagged the handles with a posting notice.

Erin knew if she did not check out this hidden entrance, she would just keep wondering about it. Besides, she wanted another chance to look inside the house. Finding a long stick lying nearby, Erin brushed away the webs and cautiously moved down the steps.

The door was solid, strong enough to protect against intruders. She tried the knob which turned with ease. But the door refused to move. With one hand turning the knob, Erin put her shoulder against the grimy door and shoved. With continued pressure, it slowly inched open and then swung inward with a loud crash. Sunshine, lighting the basement floor, poured in around her. She moved in far enough to see what had caused the crashing noise. A large steamer trunk lay on its side with the drawers pulled out and the contents strewn in haste. Empty wooden packing boxes were sprawled at random across the floor. The rifled drawers had been abandoned by the intruder, but the packing boxes were empty and appeared untouched until Erin pushed them down to open the door.

The sunlight on the basement floor provided plenty of light to find her way as she moved up the stairs.

Everything looked much the same as it had on Thursday when she had discovered the break-in. Moving cautiously, she stepped over piles of books and paper. Pictures hung crookedly on the walls. Others were lying on the floor with their glass and frames broken. Apparently the intruder had looked behind them and then just let them fall. Every carpet was pulled aside, just as Robert had mentioned at dinner last evening. In the bedrooms, mattresses were pushed off their box springs. Every drawer was open and the contents rifled or spilled onto the floor.

It was eerie to be in the middle of all this, and she was becoming uneasy about her intrusion. Moving quickly, she returned to the living room where she stopped, staring at a large secretary standing against the far wall. The front leaf was down. Small inside drawers were lying on the writing surface. The desk, similar to the one at her mother's house, shone with polished cherry wood and bright brass fixtures.

Suddenly, in the coolness of the house, she shuddered. Her desire to search for some unknown object evaporated. She decided it was time to leave. Closing the hall door to the basement, she descended the stairs. On the bottom step, she froze. There was a sound of movement coming from the outside entrance. Her heart began to pound. Suddenly, filled with visions of a killer confronting her in this damp basement, a place where she wasn't supposed to be, Erin gathered her courage and quietly stepped around the packing crates and braced against the wall near the door. In the sunlight on the basement floor, she could see a shadow of movement. Erin heard a faint rustling above the concrete steps. Had the intruder returned? Her heart was beating faster now. The next few seconds seemed like an eternity, but nothing happened. Subtle movement was sill blocking part of the sunlight on the basement floor. Finally, she edged around the doorsill, her mind projecting the image of an assailant, weapon poised, ready to do her in. Then she cried out, "Oh my god! You frightened me to death!"

Rolf was sitting just outside the top step, his tongue hanging out, softly panting as he peered down, too timid to enter the unfamiliar opening. With a sigh of relief for letting the dog panic her, she quickly closed the bottom door and hurried up the steps to replace the metal covers. Outside, the big dog seemed happy with this new game of hide-and-seek. He ran ahead barking his joy as Erin hurried back to the farmyard and climbed into the pickup.

Rolf followed her up the lane to the county road then stopped. Checking the rearview mirror as she drove away, she could see him watching. Then he turned and disappeared out of sight into the trees.

* * *

When Erin pulled into the garage, the Taylors' Buick was back, and her grandfather was in his office.

"Good morning," he said when she entered.

"Hi," she answered, lowering herself into the chair by his desk.

He was wearing a white shirt and tie, and she thought he looked quite handsome.

"Did you get my note?" he asked.

"Yes, I fed Rolf and let him loose for the day."

"Thank you, sweetheart. With the men off today I did the morning chores before we left for church." He never mentioned the dirt smudges on her cheek and sweatshirt.

"We ran into Joe Butler after services. He should be here around one o'clock for dinner. I think your grandmother is in the kitchen baking something."

"I'll go in and see if there is anything I can do to help. See you later, Gramps," Erin said. She left his office and headed for the house.

"Good morning, dear," her grandmother said, as Erin entered the kitchen.

"Hi, Gram. Can I help you with something before Mr. Butler arrives?"

"You could set the table. You have a big smudge on your face and your sweatshirt is dirty."

"Guess I did this when I went over to feed Rolf."

"I told your grandfather I didn't like him sending you over to that place."

Erin didn't mention her venture into the Lawrence farmhouse. "I'm planning to wear a dress for dinner," Erin said.

"Fine, dear," Gram responded, busy peeling potatoes at the sink. "No need to dress up too much. Joe is more family than company."

* * *

Shortly before one that afternoon, Joe Butler's car came to a gradual stop in the Taylors' farmyard.

"Hello there!" Bert called, walking to meet him as Joe slowly climbed out of a dark maroon Chrysler sedan. "Glad you were able to join us for dinner."

"You know I'd drive a long way to spend a pleasant afternoon like this with you and Florence. Especially if I'm invited to enjoy her cooking."

When they were all at the table, Bert Taylor gave the blessing and Florence began passing platters of food to their guest. Soon, Joe was busy pouring rich brown gravy over a heaping pile of mashed potatoes. It pleased Gram to watch everyone digging into her meal. After the light breakfast and her adventure at the Lawrence farm, Erin found she was hungry also.

Later, as Gram dished out apple pie and poured coffee, Bert asked Joe about his law practice.

"Busier than I would like. The last few years it seems like the work load is more than I can keep up with. I guess getting older each year doesn't help. Wish there was more I could do for some of our unfortunate farmers. Take the Jed Harper incident. I can't help feeling bad for him and his family."

"What happened?" Erin asked, pushing back her unfinished pie.

"Last fall Jed was in the field working with a corn picker. When it jammed, he tried to clear it and caught his sleeve in the chain drive. It pulled his arm into the feeder mechanism and mangled it so badly they had to amputate it."

"What could you have done, Joe?" Florence asked.

"It poses a real hardship on the family. Most farmers feel the equipment manufactures are partially to blame for these accidents. They could be providing better safety in the design of their products. Trying to prove them as even partly responsible would be difficult. It is the old story of the little guy against the big corporation. I would love to go after Consolidated Implement Company. They are the largest producer of farm equipment, and have a high incidence of injuries."

"Do you think you could build a case against them?" Bert asked.

"I'm sure there is plenty of evidence which would stand up in court showing they are lax if not negligent about making safer equipment. But getting them before a jury would be a costly challenge."

"I know what you would be up against," said Erin. "The work involved for a lawsuit like that would be expensive and time-consuming."

"You're familiar with this type of litigation?" Joe asked her.

"A couple of years back our firm represented a class action suit against a tool and die company in which several of their workers suffered injuries on dangerous equipment."

"How did it come out?" Bert asked.

"We were able to convince a jury the company had ignored repeated warnings about safety issues and won the suit for the workers."

"Were you involved in the case?" Joe asked

"I helped on most of the pre-trial depositions and discovery work with a team of experts we used as witnesses. It took four months to compile what we needed, and the time spent in court took another two months."

"What did the jury give those poor men?" Florence asked.

"At the time it was one of the largest personal injury awards in the state of Michigan. The total was two million, eight hundred thousand. The plaintiffs received one hundred and thirty three thousand dollars each. It was more than any of them would make in a lifetime."

"What did your firm receive?" Gram asked.

"One million, one hundred and twenty thousand dollars."

"You must have received a generous bonus for your part," Joe commented.

"No, our costs were substantial. The balance went into a reserve fund which the partners share at the end of the year."

"Aren't you a partner?" Joe asked.

"No, I'm an associate attorney and function in a support role doing background work for trial cases. It's a sore issue with me," Erin said, unable to hide her displeasure.

"Bert, why don't you and Joe go into the living room while Erin and I clear the dishes," Florence said, trying to change the mood at the table.

Later, when the two women joined the men, they talked until Joe noticed it was after six. "It's time for me to be heading back to town," he said.

Erin and her grandparents walked the old attorney to his car, then waved good-bye as Joe circled the farmyard and headed for Parkston.

That evening, Erin joined her grandfather while they put the shepherd in for the night. She never mentioned finding an outside entrance or entering the house. On their way back home, Erin was deep in thought. She could not stop wondering what had been of such value that someone would kill Ed Lawrence and tear his house apart trying to find it.

* * *

17

When Erin and her grandfather returned from the Lawrence farm, Gram said Robert had called asking if Erin would please call him at home that evening. He had never telephoned her at the Taylors' before. She wondered if there was something important from Ted Gilbert.

Erin cranked the telephone for the operator and asked her to ring the sheriff's house. It rang several times with no answer. She was about to hang up when he answered. "Robert, this is Erin."

"Hi. I called earlier to ask if you would like to come to my place for a cookout?"

"When?" she asked.

"How does tomorrow evening around six o'clock sound?"

It surprised her that he wanted to get together so soon. "Sure, that sounds fine," she said.

"I'll be happy to pick you up at your grandparents'."

"It might be easier if I drive over to your place," she offered.

"Great. I'll look forward to seeing you then," he said.

When Erin told her grandmother about Robert's invitation, Gram said they had no plans. She should go and enjoy herself. Just then, Bert walked in. Erin mentioned wanting to use their car Monday night. He said that she was welcome to use it as they wouldn't be going out.

Later that evening, while she was preparing for bed, Erin thought about Robert's call. She enjoyed his company and was looking forward to seeing him again.

* * *

During the night, Erin dreamed she was inside the Lawrence farmhouse. *Now, all the furniture and contents intruders had strewn about were gone, and a dense fog was creeping through the house. When she entered the living room, a large secretary was standing against the wall. She stared at it for some time. A chill from the dampness seemed to penetrate. She wanted to leave. As Erin turned to go, she was startled to see Ted Gilbert was standing in the doorway glaring at her.*

"What are you doing?" he demanded. "You're not supposed to be in here, and what have you done with all the evidence?"

Erin tried to offer some explanation, but before she could respond, the FBI agent faded away leaving her alone in the cold gray mist.

Erin was suddenly awake. It was morning. For a time, she lay quietly under the covers while a breeze from the open window chilled her room. The harder she tried to recall details of her dream, the more they faded like ghosts lost to the light of day.

* * *

At six o'clock that evening, Erin parked the Taylors' car in the driveway behind Robert's house. It was the first time she had seen his place in the daylight. It appeared newly painted and looked to be in excellent condition.

Robert was busy starting up the grill on a brick patio between the house and the garage. He waved as she climbed out of the Buick and walked up the stone path to meet him.

Erin's hair was pulled back and tied with a scarf which matched her blouse open at the throat. She was wearing the same shorts she had worn that first day on the highway.

"Looking rather striking, my dear," he said, pleased to see her again.

"Thank you, sir. You're looking quite handsome this evening yourself." She did think he looked sexy, as she took in his Madras short sleeve shirt, light tan walking shorts and loafers. It was the first time she had seen his legs. They were well shaped and muscular, like his arms. When she stopped next to him, he lowered the lid on the grill and placed one arm around her waist He pulled her to him. He gave her a light kiss.

"Can I get you something to drink while the fire is heating up?"

"What are you having?" Erin asked, holding his arm as they walked toward the house.

"I was planning to have a beer. It seems to go with cooking out."

"Great thought. I'll have the same," she said as they entered the kitchen.

On the counter, there was a shallow baking dish containing two strip steaks marinating in a dark liquid.

"What do we have here, a secret sauce?" she asked, leaning against the counter.

He didn't answer but opened the refrigerator and removed two cold bottles of Schlitz. When he reached for a glass in the cupboard, Erin stopped him.

"No glass, please," she said.

He handed her the open bottle, and she tipped it up, taking a healthy swallow. "Just think of me as one of the boys."

"That would be hard to imagine," he said. "Back to your question…"

"Yes…?"

"About the sauce," he continued, "it's an old family recipe handed down from generation to generation. My grandfather made me swear never to reveal the ingredients."

"I certainly wouldn't ask you to dishonor your ancestors."

"It's Coke."

"I beg your pardon?"

"That's all it is. Coca-Cola. It breaks down the fat and helps to tenderize the meat."

"Some secret!" she responded, rolling her eyes.

"Are you hungry?" he asked.

"I'm getting there."

"Well, I'd better get busy," he said. Robert excused himself and returned to check on the grill. Erin followed him as far as the porch where she studied the small table set with a candle and some flowers from his lilac bush. The sun had fallen behind tall trees west of his yard. In a soft breeze their lightly moving branches made changing shadow patterns across the porch screen.

When the steaks were ready, Erin brought a salad bowl from the refrigerator. As she placed it on the table, an enticing odor coming from his grille told her she was hungry.

Robert asked her to take a seat and presented a plate holding the sizzling steak and a golden-brown baked potato.

Everything was delicious.

As they finished their meal, he asked about dessert.

"Oh, Robert, I couldn't eat another bite! I'm stuffed!"

Soon he returned from the kitchen with a plate of strawberry shortcake piled high with whipped cream. He placed two forks along side. "You can help me if you like, or just watch."

Before long, Erin joined him and together they consumed the generous dessert.

When they were though with coffee, the sun had set, leaving a faint red glow behind the treetops.

Robert cleaned up his grill and wheeled it back into the garage. In the house, Erin found an apron and began washing their dishes. When Robert returned, he paused at the doorway, watching her. She appeared right at home, busy at his kitchen sink.

Later in the living room, they sat together on the sofa and talked in the quiet of the evening. Erin mentioned her grandparents had invited Joe Butler for dinner on Sunday. "He seems like a dedicated and caring person. During the meal, he expressed wanting to help families of injured men hurt while working with dangerous farm equipment."

"I know how he feels," Robert agreed. "I've been at too many of those accidents and they're tragic. They hurt people struggling to make a living. Now there is a cause you could champion."

"Thanks for the confidence, but something like this would involve a major lawsuit, and my trial experience is limited."

"I'll bet you would be great in court," Robert said.

His comment surprised Erin because he knew little about her work as a lawyer. She assumed her grandfather had been bragging again.

As the evening progressed, they shared more details of their personal lives. Erin told him about her childhood, and how she missed never knowing her paternal grandparents who had died while her father was still in law school. She related the times when she listened to her father and Uncle Maxwell talk about court trials, and how it influenced her to attend law school. She even told Robert about her stuffed animal collection and playing on the tennis team in high school and at Kalamazoo College.

For the first time, Robert was more open, telling her about his parents who had a small farm west of Parkston. His father only had a sixth grade education and worked hard all his life. It was a blow to their small family when he died of cancer at the age of forty-five. At the time of his death, Robert was twelve and their only child. Afterward his mother had been forced to sell the farm and buy a small place in town. They had barely enough to get by on through the years, yet his mother had insisted he receive a proper education. She had taken the bus to Iowa City so she could be there when he graduated from the University. His mother was fifty-six when she died, two months before he entered the service.

It annoyed Erin hearing how his fiancée, Sharon Milton, had written him breaking off their engagement during his recovery in a military hospital. As he talked, she could tell these were painful memories and didn't press him further.

The evening slipped into night as they talked. When the grandfather clock in the hall chimed once for the half hour, Erin asked about the time.

"Eleven-thirty," Robert answered.

"Well, I guess Cinderella better get herself on the road before the clock strikes twelve and she turns into a pumpkin."

"I think it was the carriage that turns into a pumpkin," he added, smiling.

"Oh yes, I remember now. Cinderella turns into a mouse," Erin said, feeling giddy and laughing at her own little joke.

On the moon-drenched rear porch, Robert pulled her into his arms. As he held her close, she willingly melted against him. There was a sense neither one wanted to let go when he said. "I could hold you like this forever."

Her only reply was to give him a tender kiss. Then she broke away." If we don't stop I'll be spending the night in your bed," she murmured in his ear.

"Can we keep that thought until another time?" he whispered back.

She didn't respond, but the look in her eyes told him the answer.

Arm and arm they walked to her car. In the clear night sky, a million stars watched as he held her one last time.

* * *

When Erin parked in the garage and walked to the house, there was a distant flash of lightning and the faint rumble of thunder.

After washing up, she slipped into bed and turned out the nightstand lamp, still immersed in thoughts of the evening with Robert. As she closed her eyes, iridescent hands on a bedside clock indicated the time with an eerie green glow. It was a quarter past midnight.

* * *

18

Erin was alone at the kitchen table, finishing the last of her breakfast. Outside, the sky was dark, and she could hear the rain falling in a steady beat on the back porch roof. It was almost nine o'clock Tuesday morning. Her grandparents had left for Spencer. Gramps had said something about looking at new farm machinery, and Florence wanted to attend a sale at Waldon's department store. They didn't plan to return until sometime in the early afternoon.

Erin's thoughts drifted to the Lawrence farmhouse and her finding the outside cellar entrance. She remembered Robert didn't want her to be over there alone.

She wondered again what the reclusive man had that was so valuable. Was it still waiting for someone to find it? Erin recalled her dream Sunday night about Ted Gilbert and the secretary-bookcase standing alone in the room. She remembered as a little girl hiding pennies in the false compartment in the secretary that was still at her mother's. *Since the desk at the Lawrence place appeared similar to the one at home, it could have a false compartment also,* she thought. Erin tried to recall how the desk front looked, but the detail escaped her. The more she thought about it, the more determined she became to check it out.

She dashed upstairs for a quick shower and dressed in a clean pair of jeans, an old long sleeved flannel shirt she had borrowed from Gramps, and her sneakers. Grabbing a light jacket against the damp morning, she hurried down the stairs, She stopped at the kitchen door. The keys to the Buick were on the hook. Her grandparents had taken the pickup.

The sky was overcast, but it was no longer raining. As she walked to the garage, she could see the barn's main doors were open and heard voices. Moving in their direction, she found Sonny and Hank inside working on a large field tractor. They both looked up when she entered.

"Good morning, gentleman," Erin called out.

"Good morning," Sonny answered.

Hank echoed the same greeting.

"I wondered if anyone has been over to feed Rolf today?" she asked.

Sonny stood up from his crouched position by the tractor and wiped his grease covered hands on an old rag. "No, not yet, Miss Hays. We've been busy since early this morning trying to get this thing running again."

"Bert told us to go over and feed him, but we got caught up in our work and didn't get to it yet," Hank added.

"I'd be happy to feed him," Erin offered.

"If you wouldn't mind, it would sure help us out," Sonny said.

Erin was pleased for an excuse to justify returning to the Lawrence farm.

* * *

While the hungry shepherd was busy devouring his food, Erin headed around the house. She barely noticed the wet lilac brushing against her shirt and jeans as she pushed past it in her eagerness to lift the metal covers hiding the outside basement steps.

They opened more easily this time, and she was soon standing in front of the large secretary. The writing leaf was down, and abandoned drawers from inside the desk looked just as before. The small door that closed over a center compartment was open and empty. On each side of it were two pillar-shaped carvings. The desk at her mother's home had similar sculptures disguising small narrow vertical drawers behind them. Erin's pulse quickened as she grasped the edges of the small pillar on the right and pulled. Nothing happened. She tried again, this time with more effort. It still wouldn't move. Doubts crossed her mind. She began to think these little wooden columns were just a solid part of the desk. Erin moved to the one on the left. With the first try, it easily slid forward and came out, but the drawer was empty.

Carefully replacing it, she gave the one on the right side another try. It still didn't move. Frustrated, she used both hands, this time positioning them at the top and bottom of the tiny pillars. With more effort, she gave it a tug. Suddenly it came free, moving out so quickly it fell from her grasp and something inside dropped onto the writing leaf with a loud thud. She stared down at the object.

A package, wrapped in heavy dark brown paper, lay on the desktop. It was about a half inch thick by six inches long and three inches wide. In the center, where the edges of the heavy brown paper came together, was a bright red seal. Imbedded in the wax imprint was an eagle perched on a wreath surrounding a swastika. She knew it was a German symbol of some kind. Her pulse quickened as she stared down at it. Finally, using the shirt cuff, she returned the package into the false compartment and slid it back into its opening. Quickly she retraced her movements to the outside steps and closed the iron doors.

Back in the Buick, Erin trembled with excitement at her discovery. Was this the mysterious prize that cost Edward Lawrence his life? What did the strange package contain? These unanswered questions were pulling at her mind. For a long while, Erin stared out the car window. She watched as Rolf chased a frightened rabbit that dashed across the farmyard. In seconds they both disappeared out of sight behind one of the out buildings.

As the elation of her discovery waned, Erin knew she had to let Robert know about the package. Yet, she was reluctant to tell him she had been entering the house to search for something based on a hunch from a dream. If the package turned out to be nothing of importance, he would think she was an idiot for ignoring the federal warnings just to satisfy her own curiosity. With a sigh, she started the car and drove through rain puddles on the lane. She headed for Parkston.

* * *

"Good morning. Is the Sheriff in?" Erin asked, approaching the reception counter.

"Good morning, Miss Hays," said Sara. "Yes, he's in his office. Please go on back."

Erin thanked the dispatcher and feeling anxious, moved slowly toward his open door. Robert was at his desk busy reading when she stopped just inside. He looked up and smiled, then stood to greet her.

"Well, good morning! What a pleasant surprise!"

She closed the door and sat down in a chair facing his desk. He saw her serious look and wondered why she had stopped by.

"I hope it will continue to be pleasant when I tell you what I have done," she said.

His expression became more serious as he waited for her to continue.

"I may have found what the intruder was looking for," she said.

His eyes narrowed. "What did you find?"

"A small sealed package."

"Did you open it?

"No."

"Where did you find it?"

"Hidden in the secretary at the Lawrence farmhouse."

Robert was silent again. She had no idea what he was thinking. His tone had been direct. She wondered if that was how he sounded when questioning a suspect.

"How did you get in the house? Wasn't it locked?"

"I found an outside entrance to the basement hidden behind some bushes. The State Crime Lab must have missed it because empty packing boxes blocked the door from the inside.

"Erin, why didn't you call me before going into the house?" he asked. His voice sounded stern.

Erin was becoming defensive. "Robert, I understand your concern. If I told you I had a dream that might lead to what the intruder was looking for, well, it would have sounded stupid."

He didn't respond, just looked at her, waiting. It was the first time there had been any words between them. It made her feel uneasy, but she remained determined. "Look, I'm being candid with you," she continued. "This could be important, and I came directly here to ask for your help. I'm well aware about what it meant entering the Lawrence house. If what I found turns out to be some essential evidence, then maybe it will justify my actions. Would you please go with me to check it out yourself?"

Robert was quiet again, and his silence made her even more

apprehensive. He fiddled with a paperweight on his desk. Abruptly, he stood up. "All right, let's go see what you found."

* * *

A short time later they were in the sheriff's county cruiser driving through the wet grove. They stopped in the Lawrence farmyard. When they stepped out of the car, Rolf was nowhere in sight. Erin assumed he was out in the fields and hadn't heard them arrive.

Together they walked around the house, and Erin showed Robert the outside entrance. They made their way into the basement. A moment later, they stood in front of the secretary. Everything was just as she had left it.

Erin pointed out the carvings that disguised the false compartments. Robert, using a pair of gloves, pulled where Erin had indicated. As he carefully eased the hidden drawer from its place in the desk, the little compartment slipped from his grasp and dropped once again on the writing surface to reveal the package. For a time, they both stared at the bright red seal with the swastika in the center.

"Do you know what the emblem is?" she asked.

"I have seen this insignia before," Robert said, now intrigued by her discovery. "It's a symbol used by Hitler's elite SS corps."

Erin did not respond, just watched as he looked around the array of papers on the floor until he found an empty manila envelope. Carefully, with his gloved hand, he pushed the mysterious package inside.

"Let's head back to my office and find out what you discovered." There was a note of anticipation in his voice.

It relieved Erin to see Robert's behavior had changed. Now he appeared to have little concern about her entry into the house.

Closing the outside basement entrance, they returned to his patrol car and headed down the winding lane. At the county road, Robert turned north toward town.

Once the patrol car was out of sight, a dark green Chevrolet sedan emerged from a secluded spot in the grove. At the end of the lane, it turned south.

* * *

As they entered the reception area, Robert asked Deputy Wilson to join them in his office. He laid the envelope on the table and suggested they all be seated.

"John, this contains a package from the Lawrence Farm. You will be a third witness when I open it."

"Sure, Chief," his deputy said, pleased for the opportunity to be included.

Again wearing his gloves, Robert removed the package. Using a penknife, he carefully slit along the package's edge, leaving its seal unbroken and pulled back the wrapping. It's contents were covered with some kind of protective coating.

"They're just a couple of greasy metal plates!" the deputy exclaimed, sounding disappointed.

Using the tip of his knife, the sheriff lifted the top plate and turned it over. The three stared at the two silver objects. They tried to see beyond the dark substance obscuring the engraved design. The only sound in the room was a fly as it buzzed around an overhead light.

After gently scraping away some of the coating with his knife, Robert broke the silence. "What we have here is the front and back engravings of a United States one-hundred-dollar bill."

No one said anything. Deputy Wilson stared at the plates in awe. He had never seen a hundred dollar bill.

Robert moved to his desk and pressed the intercom for Sara. He wanted to put in a call for Ted Gilbert.

"How do these plates fit in with the Lawrence killing?" the deputy asked.

"I can't answer you, John, but someone wanted them badly enough to risk several years in jail."

It was not long before Sara's voice on the intercom said Agent Gilbert was on the line. Robert picked up the telephone and explained that Erin had discovered a package in the Lawrence farmhouse and what it contained.

"Yes, the plates will be in my safe until the State Police come for them. Right. I'll tell her." He replaced the receiver and turned to Erin. "Well, you don't need to be concerned about entering the house. Gilbert said to tell you thanks for your good work on discovering the plates."

Erin felt relief now that the agent had given his approval of her unauthorized intrusions.

"I don't get it. What was the Lawrence guy doing with these plates?"

asked Deputy Wilson. "Did he steal them from somebody who wanted them back badly enough to kill him?"

"The FBI will have to deal with those questions," Robert told him.

* * *

19

The day's improving weather mirrored Erin's mood as she drove south of Parkston on US 59 heading back to the Taylors' farm. The bright June sun warmed her through the car's windows. It was a relief knowing Ted Gilbert had little if any concern over her unauthorized exploring in the Lawrence house.

She wondered about Edward Lawrence. Robert had passed along news from Gilbert that his body was in Sioux City, and they were waiting for the pathologist's autopsy report. There was still no information on his suspected killer. A puzzle with too many missing pieces. *Maybe the forged plates will help to fill in some of the picture and lead to finding Gus Mann,* she thought.

As Erin neared the entrance to the Taylors' farm, a rabbit darted across the road and disappeared into a cornfield. It reminded her of Rolf chasing one earlier that morning. *Strange,* Erin thought, *when Robert and I returned, the shepherd was nowhere in sight.* The big dog always came barking whenever she entered the property. *It could be he was after something and was too far from the house to hear the sound of Robert's car.* After parking in the garage, she dismissed her concern over Rolf's failing to show up.

* * *

It was a little past noon when Erin sat at the kitchen table eating a sandwich. Gram had left it wrapped in wax paper and placed on a shelf in the refrigerator. Her grandparents still had not returned from their trip to Spencer. Later, while folding some clean clothes, she thought again about Rolf. It still bothered her, his not showing up this morning. Feeling that something wasn't right, she returned to the Buick and headed for Edward Lawrence's farm.

There was no sign of him when she stopped near the house. Standing outside the car, she reached through the open window and honked the horn and waited. The only response came from a flock of crows somewhere in the distance.

Erin walked toward the barn and scanned across acres of unplanted fields. She repeatedly called Rolf's name. Erin even managed a healthy, two fingered whistle. There was no response.

Walking to the barn, she entered the separator room. Light inside was dim. It took awhile for her vision to adjust. After a moment, she could make out the shepherd lying on a straw bed where he slept at night. Bending down, she touched him and could detect his shallow breathing. It was if he were asleep. Erin noticed dog chow scattered nearby on the barn's planked flooring. There was a strange medicinal odor coming from the food. At once she knew something was seriously wrong. When a loud fluttering noise broke the silence, Erin froze. Looking up she saw a pigeon fleeing from a nest in the rafters. "Take it easy," she mumbled under her breath. "It is just a noisy bird." As she turned her attention back to the unmoving dog, she heard a creaking noise just behind her. She started to turn. A sharp pain penetrated the side of her head. Everything faded into darkness. She slumped to the floor.

* * *

When Erin regained consciousness, her head was throbbing. She tried raising her hand, but it wouldn't respond. Slowly she realized someone had tied her hands and feet to a chair. Tight ropes were binding her. They hurt when she tried to move, but it was nothing like the pounding in her head. Through half-closed eyes, she could see two men sitting close together just across from her at a table.

"What do you expect to find out if she is unconscious and can't talk?" said someone off to the side.

"Be quiet! I know how to deal with this. She is coming around now."

Erin struggled to focus. Slowly, the vision of two men merged into one person. He was glaring at her. Now any sense of physical discomfort faded in a rush of terror as she recognized him. The sinister individual facing her was the same one she had identified as the possible killer of Edward Lawrence, Gus Mann! the hoodlum from Chicago!

"Well, my dear Miss Hays, how nice to see you again," he uttered in a patronizing tone. His words were laced with traces of a German accent.

"What do you think you are doing!" she blurted out in defiance, then winced. Raising her voice had magnified the ache in her head.

"Now, now, Miss Hays. Hostility will not help. We know you and your sheriff friend removed something from the house this morning. Just tell me what you found and where it is, please." His voice was lower, but still threatening. It matched his huge physical presence.

"I don't know what you're talking about," she said, this time lowering her voice to lessen the pain.

"Kidnapping is a federal offense," Erin said, in desperation

"Don't play games with me, or you may not live to be concerned about federal charges or anything else!" roared Mann. His tone was angry now. He appeared even more menacing as he scowled at her.

A second man walked around from behind Erin and took a chair at the table. He was tall and slender with thick dark hair combed straight back. The look on his face was less intimidating. She had never seen him before.

"Maybe she doesn't know what we want," the second man said.

"Shut up! She knows, and I plan to get it out of her," Mann said, his voice booming in the room Erin now recognized as the kitchen of the Lawrence farmhouse.

Erin was desperately trying to stay focused. She had to convince them she didn't know what they were after.

"I was looking for a deed to the farm," Erin said, her voice strained and weak. "I needed the sheriff to legally enter the house. We found it, and the sheriff decided to hold everything for the probate judge." Erin was trying to sound convincing, while wincing in pain as she talked.

"Liar!" He yelled at her so loudly she flinched. "You are through wasting our time!"

He turned to the second man. "Go ahead and inject her," he ordered.

His partner rose from the table and moved to the kitchen counter.

He returned with a small black case. He removed a hypodermic syringe and a tiny bottle containing a clear liquid. Pushing the syringe into the vial, he pulled back the plunger. When it filled, he depressed the plunger until the fluid squirted into the air.

Erin stiffened as he approached and pulled up the sleeve of her grandfather's flannel shirt. She strained against the ropes in a futile gesture of resistance as the needle entered her arm.

"Now," Mann said, his voice lower and not as threatening, "there will be no more lies, just the truth this time."

Erin was beginning to panic. "What have you done to me?" she pleaded, her voice trembling.

"Just a little something to improve our communication, my dear." While Mann spoke, the drug flowed through her veins, its warmth melting away the pain as she drifted into a state of calm. She could feel herself floating away from the danger.

Mann leaned over the table, "Now, Miss Hays, let us go back to this morning. What were you and the sheriff doing in the house?"

She struggled, trying to focus on her story about the property deed. "Looking for deed in desk." Her words came out broken and slurred.

"See, I thought she was telling the truth," his partner said.

"Be quiet, Fritz!" Mann snapped. Then, his voice became calm and friendly. "Miss Hays, tell me about the people on the next farm."

"Grandparents..."

"Good. Now, why are you living with them?"

"Visiting..." Her voice was almost a whisper.

"Tell me why you continued coming here each day."

"To feed dog.. Owner killed… No one to care for shepherd."

"Did you bring the sheriff here today to feed the dog?"

"No… To search desk."

"What for?" Mann kept his voice low and steady.

"Looking for something…" Erin paused, confused. "Put deed in big envelope."

"She didn't find them after all," the man with the dark hair said.

"Will you be quiet?" Mann growled, then turned back to Erin.

"Why did you leave?

"Found package with silver plates..."

"Damn it! They found them!" Mann stood and began pacing the floor around Erin's chair.

She tried to watch him, but it seemed as if she were dreaming.

"When you left with the sheriff, what did you do?" Mann asked.

"Drove to office...locked in safe...," Erin said, barely conscious.

"What'll we do now, Gus?" You know how the mob is about screwing things up. The cops have the plates and Santini will be mad as hell about all this."

"Goddamnit. Fritz! Quit whining. Shut the hell up and let me think!" Mann was on his feet and started to pace the kitchen floor. "The only chance we have is to use the woman. Maybe we can trade her for the plates. This hick town sheriff might be just dumb enough to do it."

"It sounds too risky. I say we cut our losses and head back to Chicago," Fritz said.

"Forget it! I'm not leaving without those plates! Put her car out of sight and bring ours close to the house. I want to get moving before someone comes nosing around."

Erin was in a fog, unaware Mann had cut the ropes binding her arms and legs. She had a sense of rising from the chair and floating down porch steps.

In the farmyard, Mann carried Erin to the rear of their car.

"Bring the keys and open the trunk," Mann told his reluctant partner, Fritz Adel.

"Are you going to put her in there?" Fritz asked.

"What do you want to do, go driving around with her in the backseat? Stop with your stupid questions. Open it!"

With Erin in their car's trunk, the two men headed out and turned south on the county road.

Deputy Wilson was less than a mile from the Lawrence farm driving north. He was returning from an accident call when he met a late model dark green Chevrolet. As they passed, he didn't recognize either of the two men in the car, but he did notice its Illinois license plate.

* * *

20

Florence Taylor was returning from upstairs when she heard the porch screen door slam shut. She thought it might be her granddaughter but Bert entered. "Have you seen anything of Erin?" she asked.

"No, I haven't," he answered, looking in the refrigerator for a pitcher of iced tea. "Why do you ask?"

"I didn't see her in town when we stopped at the grocery on our way back from Spencer. We've been home some time now, and I'll bet she's at the Lawrence place again. You know I don't like her going there. I wish this whole mess would just go away."

"I wouldn't get too worked up. She's a big girl and can take care of herself," Bert replied, removing a glass from the cupboard.

"Big girl or not, I'd feel better if you would drive over to see what's keeping her so long."

"All right. Just let me finish my tea first," Bert grumbled.

* * *

"Fifteen minutes later, Erin's grandfather pulled his pickup to a stop in the Lawrence farmyard. There was no sign of the Buick. The place was quiet, and Rolf was nowhere in sight. He stepped from the pickup and called for the Shepherd. When there was no response, Bert decided to check the barn. He thought Erin might have put him there for some reason.

When Bert entered the separator room, he found the shepherd lying on the straw bed. Rolf raised his head and whimpered. "What's the matter, boy?" Bert said, kneeling down beside him. The dog tried to

122

raise himself but slumped back down and whined. Bert gently stroked the animal wondering what was the matter with him when he noticed Rolf's food scattered on the floor and detected its strange odor. Scooping some of the dog chow with his hand, he smelled it. At once, he knew it wasn't right. Something had contaminated the food. The dog was drugged.

Bert left the separator room door open to let in fresh air and quickly headed for the house. When he reached for the kitchen doorknob, he could see a splintered sill where someone had forced it. Inside, he saw a chair pulled back from the table with clothesline rope lying on the floor. Alarmed, he called out for his granddaughter. There was no answer. He hurried from room to room, even checked the basement, but Erin was not there.

Back outside, he called her name and waited for an answer. There was none. As he scanned the farmyard and outbuildings for some sign of Erin, he caught a glimpse of something bright coming from the barn's far side. Moving quickly, he found the Buick parked just out of sight. If the sun had not reflected off the car's chrome bumper at just the right angle, he would never have noticed it. Nervously, he checked inside. There was nothing but her jacket, lying in the backseat. The keys were still in the ignition. He took them and moved to the trunk, afraid of what he might find. It was empty.

Bert hurried back to the house and looked in the hallway for the telephone. He fought to catch enough breath to talk. He hastily turned the crank to ring the operator. It seemed she would never answer. Then, suddenly, she was on the line.

"This is Bert Taylor. Please ring the sheriff's office!" he shouted into the phone.

"Sorry, Bert. Both lines are busy."

"Well, cut in anyway!"

"I can't do that, only in case of an emergency."

"Damn it! This is an emergency! Just do it!" Bert Taylor hardly ever swore.

"Okay, Bert, just keep your shirt on," the operator snapped and plugged into the sheriff's dispatch line.

Sara was talking to her son.

"Sorry to break in, Sara. I have Bert Taylor on the line. He says it's an emergency."

"Yes, Bert. What is it?" Sara asked.

"I'm at the Lawrence farm. Erin has disappeared, and there is something very wrong over here. Please send someone right away! I'm afraid she may have been kidnapped!" A chill went through him at the sound of his own words.

"Deputy Wilson should be somewhere in your area. I'll contact him at once. Please wait there until he arrives."

"I will. Please tell him to hurry." Bert was trembling as he replaced the receiver back on it's hook.

It wasn't long before a patrol car skidded to a halt in the farmyard.

"What happened?" John Wilson called to Bert as he sprang from the cruiser.

"Come with me," Bert answered, heading toward the rear porch. As they reached the steps, another patrol car raced down the lane, flew into the farmyard and came to an abrupt stop. A long radio antenna attached to its bumper whipped back and forth through the air. The car door flew open. Sheriff Thomas jumped out.

Once inside the house, they saw the chair and ropes, then rapidly searched again for some sign of Erin. When they found nothing, Bert led them to the Buick. Sheriff Thomas felt the hood, It was cool. The car had not been driven for some time.

After checking on the dog, they stood together in the farmyard. Sheriff Thomas asked if Bert had heard or seen something out of the ordinary.

"No I can't recall anything."

"Have you noticed any strangers in the area lately?"

"No, I haven't," Bert replied.

"Wait a minute!" Deputy Wilson broke in, "About two hours ago I was driving north, on the road that passes by here. I met a car with two men in it. Never saw either of them before."

"Describe the car," the sheriff said, reflecting urgency in his voice.

"It was a late model Chevy, a four-door sedan, dark green, with an Illinois license plate."

"Did you get a good enough look at the two men to describe them?"

"No sir. They were moving too fast."

"Anybody else in the car?"

"As near as I could tell, it was just the two men."

"Good work spotting the car's plate, John."

Robert remembered that after Erin identified Gus Mann, the FBI teletype associated him with a Chicago mob. His deputy spotting the Illinois plate gave them something to work on.

"You stay here and hold anyone who shows up. Keep Sara informed."

"Right, Chief."

"Bert, you might as well go home. If anything turns up, I'll call you," Robert said, doing his best to hide any sign of the deep concern he had for Erin.

Seated in his patrol car, Robert radioed Sara instructions to call the State Police and give them a description of the car with Illinois plates. "Place a call to Ted Gilbert and tell him about Erin." After Robert signed off, he quickly departed.

Bert and the deputy watched as the sheriff's cruiser threw a shower of dirt from its tires as he sped up the lane.

Bert Taylor lingered for a time, then climbed into his pickup and headed back home. After parking in the garage, he hesitated once more, dreading the thought of telling Florence his news about their granddaughter.

* * *

21

In the car's dark trunk, Erin was beginning to regain some control. Still frightened, but even more, she was angry, and it helped to clear her head. Only vaguely aware of what she had said to her abductors in the farmhouse kitchen, she recalled something about looking for the farm's property deed. Erin could not remember how she ended up in a car's trunk, or even whose car it was.

She rubbed her sore wrists and ankles where the ropes had pulled tight against them. Trying to ignore the queasy feeling in her stomach, she found it difficult to orient herself in the moving darkness. *At least I'm not tied,* Erin thought, aware the longer she could manage to stay alive, the better her chance to escape.

Trying to listen over tire noise from the pavement, she could hear the muffled sounds of conversation but couldn't make out what was being said. It was impossible to tell how much time had passed. The car continued to move in a direction unknown to her.

* * *

Sometime later, when they finally stopped and turned the engine off, Erin could hear their voices more clearly.

Mann was talking to his partner. "As long as she is unconscious we'll leave her in the trunk. When it gets dark, we can move her out of sight into our cabin."

"I still don't like this," Fritz grumbled. "We should have left her at the farmhouse and cleared out for Chicago."

"We're not leaving until we get those plates!" Mann's gruff voice seemed more determined than ever. "Go in the cabin and pull the shades!"

She could hear both car doors open and close and then the sound of a screen door slamming shut. Erin remained quiet until she was sure they had gone inside.

In the trunk's hot, confined space, she felt nauseated from the drug, and her head ached. The possibility they might decide to kill her heightened Erin's resolve. She must find a way to free herself.

* * *

In the motel's small office, Freddie Summers, the day clerk, was posting room charges from guests who had checked out.

On the counter, a small radio was about to finish the local five o'clock report. "That's news and weather for tomorrow," then the announcer paused... "This item just in... The State Police are asking anyone who has seen two men in a late model, dark green Chevrolet with Illinois license plates, to call their local law enforcement agency. These men are wanted for questioning on possible kidnapping charges. They should be considered armed and dangerous! Now, we continue with the swinging sounds of Ray Anthony and his orchestra. This is station KCKI in Cherokee."

The music filled the small office as Freddie finished his accounting work and closed a nearby filing cabinet. Turning to the counter, Freddie noticed the motel's registration book. Something prompted him to open it and turn back a few pages to an entry for the only guests still occupying a cabin. The scrawled, barely legible names were "G. Jones" and. "F. Smith," with both addresses given as Chicago, Illinois.

Freddie recalled when the two men registered, they had requested a cabin away from the highway. They said they wanted quiet. He was sure their car was a dark color, maybe green. He stepped outside and looked down the row of single units where he could just make out the rear of their car parked on the far side of their cabin. He continued moving and cautiously approached it. The shades were down; there was no sound from inside. After a quick glance at the late model Chevy, he hurried back to the office.

* * *

When Bert Taylor returned home, he sat quietly in his pickup to compose himself before heading to the house.

"Did you find Erin?" his wife asked, as he slowly entered the kitchen.

"Erin is missing."

"What do you mean missing?" she said. Her voice wavered.

As softly and calmly as he could manage, he explained what he had discovered at the Lawrence farm and told her about calling for Deputy Wilson and the arrival of Sheriff Thomas.

"Oh, no!" she exclaimed, starting to cry.

Bert put his arm around her shaking shoulders and helped her into a chair at the kitchen table.

"This is terrible! What will we do?" she sobbed.

"All we can do is hope and pray she's all right. Erin's a smart girl, and I'm sure she'll somehow manage to find a way to deal with whoever took her." Then, unable to hold back his own emotion, tears began to spill down *his* weathered cheeks.

* * *

Erin's eyes were becoming adjusted to the dark trunk, and she could just make out the dim shape of her confined space. She probed quietly for anything she could use to help her escape. In a far corner her hand closed over what felt like an iron rod. In the faint light, she could just make out its L shape. Her own car had a tire changing kit, and she was sure this one was similar and used to loosen the nuts holding the tires. What she wanted was the end designed to pry off the hubcaps. Erin hoped she could use it to jimmy the trunk lid. Lying on her left side, she felt around the latch. She looked for a place to insert the flat end of the wrench. At the sound of a screen door slamming and heavy footsteps crunching on the gravel, she froze. As the footsteps sounded nearer, she quickly rolled over with her back to the opening and placed the wrench out of sight in front of her. Keeping still, she heard the sound of someone inserting a key. When the trunk lid opened, Erin could feel a rush of fresh air. *I've got to convince them I'm still drugged,* she thought.

"Wake up!" Mann's gravelly voice commanded.

Erin's heart was pounding She felt like it would explode as she fought to keep still.

He reached in and roughly shook her. "Can't you hear me? I said wake up!"

It took every ounce of concentration for her to remain limp. For what seem like an endless time, he continued to stand silently outside the trunk. Then, he mumbled, "Good," and closed the lid.

Erin remained motionless until she heard the screen door open and close. There was no sound of movement outside the car. *I've got to get out of here!* she thought, feeling a renewed sense of desperation.

Again facing the trunk lid, she felt for a place on the latch where she could insert the lug wrench. Finding a spot she hoped might work, Erin held the bar with both hands, braced herself, and pushed down with all her strength. Just as a tiny crack of light appeared, the bar slipped from the opening, and slammed down striking her knuckles on the trunk floor. "Damn!" she cried in an outburst of pain. She touched the backs of her stinging hands. They were wet and sticky with blood. Tears of frustration spilled from her eyes a she lay sweating in the darkness.

* * *

22

A State Trooper had been patrolling on Route 3, one mile east of Marcus, Iowa, when he received a call directing him to the Shady Cabins Motel, two miles south of Cherokee. The dispatcher gave him details on the kidnapping suspects and advised that he approach with caution. The trooper estimated his time of arrival would be sixteen minutes.

* * *

At a drive-in restaurant on route 31 in the village of Quimby, a Cherokee County deputy was finishing a sandwich when his short wave radio crackled to life. The call gave him limited information about two suspects at the Shady Cabins Motel, and ordered him to the location. He was to hold his position outside until the arrival of a state trooper now en route. The deputy knew Freddie and told his dispatcher he would be there in approximately ten minutes.

* * *

In the Chevy's trunk, Erin wiped away her tears with the sleeve of her grandfather's shirt. Anger at the captors filled her with stubborn resolve. She groped along the trunk floor for the elusive lug wrench. Finding it, she wedged the flat end in the same place near the latch and pulled down with all the strength she could muster. A sliver of light appeared but nothing happened. Suddenly, a sharp metallic snap filled her ears as the lid flew open. She found herself exposed to cool air and bright sunlight.

Erin didn't move, listening for any sign that her captors had heard the noise. The only sound was from a breeze rustling leaves on a nearby tree and the distant highway noise of a truck somewhere down from the motel.

She quickly stumbled out and stood up for the first time. Feeling sore and cramped, she squinted in the bright sunlight, trying to orient herself. She glanced toward the cabin, where she assumed her captors were inside. The door appeared closed, and the shades drawn. There was no sound or sign of movement inside.

Down the two rows of small whitewashed cabins, Erin could see the neon tubing of a sign spelling out the word "Office." She stepped carefully across the gravel driveway to a grass median separating the rows of cabins, then ran as fast as her stiff legs would carry her toward the sign. Reaching the office door, she frantically pushed it open and confronted the shocked day clerk. "Quick, call the police. I've been kidnapped!" From her parched throat, the words came out raspy and high-pitched. It sounded to her as if a stranger were talking.

Behind the counter, Freddie Summers stared wide-eyed at the disheveled woman. Tear stains streaked Erin's dirty face. Her tangled hair hung down in strings, the ends matted against her damp neck. The backs of her hands were scraped and smeared with dried blood.

"I d...did," he stammered, "I already called them... Ten minutes ago... It was on the radio, about a green Chevy." His jumbled words spilled out in rapid succession. "I went up to cabin twelve, checking on their car. It matched the description so I came back and called the Sheriff. They should be here any minute." A feeling of relief flowed over Erin when she realized help was on the way.

She was trying to catch her breath when the office door burst open, and Gus Mann entered, pointing a revolver at the two startled occupants.

"Down on the floor, both of you! Hands behind your heads!"

The frightened clerk started to lower himself behind the counter.

"Out here!" Mann shouted at him. "If either of you move, it will be your last!"

Erin and Freddie did as he ordered. Now stretched out face down on the hard concrete floor, Erin's heart sank at the failed attempt to escape.

Fritz Adel was standing outside their cabin waiting. Behind him, the Chevy's trunk lid was still wide open. Mann stepped partway through the open office door. He kept his gun pointed at the two hostages while motioning Adel to join him. In a moment, Erin could hear footsteps on the gravel drive as the second man approached.

Adel stopped short when he came through the door and saw there were two captives on the floor. "What will we do with them?" he asked. "This thing is getting messy."

"Close the door and find something to tie them up with," Mann ordered.

At the sound of an automobile stopping next to the office, Mann looked out through slatted blinds on the front window. He could see a patrol car with COUNTY SHERIFF in large letters across the cruiser's side.

"Get down!" Mann whispered to Adel. The two crouched low against the front wall.

The deputy stepped out and looked through the front window; however, the blinds' angle prevented him from seeing the floor. At the closed office door, he stopped and listened. He could see no one through the door's small glass window. The only sound came from the radio playing a Duke Ellington blues number. His left hand turned the knob. His right hand lifted a revolver from its holster.

"Freddie, are you in there?" He called out, slowly opening the door. When he was in far enough to see the two hostages lying on the floor, it was too late.

Mann, pressed against the wall, struck the deputy's head with his pistol. The deputy slumped forward, unconscious.

"Jesus!" Fritz said. "Now we're in for it!"

"Shut the hell up! Help me pull him behind the counter," Mann ordered. They dragged the limp body out of sight, placed him on the floor face down, and secured his arms behind him with handcuffs from the deputy's belt.

As Adel looked for something to tie up the other two hostages, the radio was making him nervous. He reached over to turn it off, but Mann told him to leave it on.

"It'll sound like everything's normal."

Then they heard a second car coming to a stop outside the office. Once again the mobsters pressed against the front wall.

Adel, closest to the window, carefully looked out between the blinds' slats. "Christ! It's another cop!" he cried.

"Damn it, Fritz! Keep your voice down." Mann hissed. No one approached the office. Mann cautiously raised his head above the windowsill just enough to see the state police unit parked behind the deputy's car. The trooper was still in the front seat.

"What's he doing?" Adel asked in a hushed voice.

"How the hell do I know? He's just sitting there," growled Mann.

Outside trooper sixty-five was assessing the situation. It didn't look right. When he had pulled to a stop, the county patrol car was still idling with the driver side door open but there was no sign of the deputy. Carefully, he opened his cruiser's door and stepped out, drawing his revolver. Quickly, he closed the distance from his car to the highway side of the office that also had a window. With his back against the wall, the trooper carefully peered inside. No one was behind the counter. The only sound came from the radio. Then he saw two people face down on the floor with their hands behind their heads.

He quickly backed away, realizing someone inside was holding them hostage. Heading to the front, he ducked under the window and stopped just short of the office entrance. Staying close to the front wall, and still holding his revolver, he reached toward the closed door with his free hand. Slowly, he turned the knob, stepped forward and kicked the door open then moved back against the outside wall.

"You in there! This is the police! Come out with your hands up!"

The only sound was the radio announcer reporting how sunny the weather would be over the next two days.

In one corner of the room, Fritz Adel, frightened and sweating, was gripping the deputy's pistol. Carefully, the state trooper started edging around the opening. When Fritz saw the trooper's hand holding a gun, he fired. The bullet missed and ripped through the door frame. The noise filled the small room with a deafening roar.

Erin winced as she lay terrified on the office floor. She could hear the young clerk softy whimpering. Her head was pounding again, and she tried not to think about her life ending here in this cheap little motel. Everything that had seemed so important only two weeks ago now seemed trivial. She desperately wanted this nightmare to go away.

"You stupid fool!" Mann spat at Adel. "What were you trying to do?"

Outside, the trooper quickly retreated to his cruiser where he grabbed the short-wave microphone. "This is unit sixty-five calling dispatch."

The radio was silent for an instant then responded. "This is dispatch. Go ahead sixty-five."

"I'm at the Shady Cabins Motel south of Cherokee. Unknown assailants holding hostages. Gunshot fired. Sheriff's deputy unaccounted for. Urgently request assistance."

"Roger, sixty-five, please stand by."

Moving forward to the open door of the deputy's cruiser, the state trooper crouched down, kept his revolver pointed at the doorway and waited.

The radio came to life again: "This is Sioux City dispatch. All available units in the vicinity of Cherokee should proceed at once for the Shady Cabins Motel on highway 59. Unit sixty-five requesting support. Hostage situation with armed assailant. Approach with extreme caution."

* * *

23

Sheriff Thomas, unable to wait helplessly in his office, was patrolling near the southern end of O'Brian county when he received a call from Sara. She radioed him the State Police had dispatched a unit to the Shady Cabins Motel one mile south of Cherokee to investigate a reported presence of two possible kidnapping suspects. Robert turned on the car's emergency lights and headed south.

* * *

Inside the motel office, the two hoodlums could hear a dispatcher on unit 65's radio directing all available patrols to their motel. In a short time the place would be swarming with police.

"We have to make a run for it," Mann said to his anxious companion. For the first time, there was the sound of confusion in the big German's voice.

"Are you insane?" Adel snapped back. "That cop will nail us cold the minute we step outside."

"Not if we use these two as a shield," Mann barked back.

Reaching down, he roughly pulled Erin up from the concrete floor. She offered little resistance against his strength. Placing her in front of him with his left arm around her waist and his right holding the pistol, he shoved her through the office doorway onto the gravel drive. Once they were both outside, Mann paused in line with the open space between the outside office wall and the deputy's abandoned patrol unit. He wanted to be sure the trooper, who was using the deputy's car door as a shield, could see the pistol at Erin's side. For a moment, all three of them stood frozen.

"Drop the gun and release the woman!" the trooper called out, his revolver leveled toward the killer and his hostage. Mann slowly edged Erin forward, moving around the deputy's cruiser. He inched toward the passenger side door. Now the car was blocking the trooper's line of fire. Erin worried if Mann would be able to shoot the officer and force her into the still running car. He might have a chance to pull off his escape, and take her with him.

A third police unit raced into the motel driveway and skidded to a stop next to the State Trooper's car. Sheriff Thomas quickly slid from behind the wheel and bent down behind the open door, his revolver drawn.

Mann stopped. With the sheriff facing him, he no longer had the deputy's car as a buffer.

Erin's mind raced. At the sight of Robert, her hopes soared and new energy surged through her trembling body.

As Mann stood motionless, Freddie Summers appeared at the doorway with Adel pushing the frightened day clerk ahead of him. In the distance, sounds of sirens pierced the air. Adel's face showed he was in near panic as he shoved his hostage forward. Just outside the door, Freddie stumbled and fell. Adel had to release his hold or go down with him. Now, Adel was directly in the line of fire from the trooper. For a split second, he was unsure of what to do. Then, he raised the deputy's revolver toward the trooper and fired. His shot went wide and careened off the office wall. Before Adel could shoot again, the police officer fired twice into Fritz Adel's chest. He was dead by the time his body slumped to the gravel drive.

The sound of the gunshots had distracted Mann. For a second he turned his attention toward the two men now down on the drive. With her eyes locked on Robert's, Erin made a subtle motion looking to her left. Robert gave a slight nod to indicate he understood. Before Mann could refocus, Erin twisted from her captor's grasp and lunged for the grass median. As she fell away, Mann's revolver instantly fired toward Sheriff Thomas. A volley of gunshots filled the air.

Erin, lying face down on the grass, was afraid to open her eyes. The only sounds she could hear came from the motel's radio and wailing sirens.

"Are you all right?" the familiar voice said. Erin looked up and saw Robert bending down next to her.

"Now I am," she answered, her voice choked with emotion. When he helped her up she threw her arms around him. She was thrilled to be alive and hoped the most terrifying day of her life was over.

Gus Mann was lying motionless on the stone driveway. The hefty German was dead. There were two bullet holes in the sheriff's car door, just inches from where Robert had been while shooting at Mann.

* * *

In a short time, the motel was swarming with police and emergency personnel. A county ambulance driver attended to Erin's bruised knuckles. He suggested transporting her to the hospital for head x-rays. The Cherokee County Deputy was sitting in the office, holding an ice bag on a lump just above his ear, sorry he didn't hold his position and wait as ordered. At the counter, the state trooper was making notes for his report. Freddie was pacing up and down outside the motel office puffing on a cigarette and babbling to anyone who would listen. The bodies of the two mobsters were on their way to the morgue.

* * *

At a hospital in Cherokee, the x-rays showed there was no fracture from Erin's hit on the head. Robert called the Taylors letting them know their granddaughter was all right and he would be bringing her home.

A short time later, Erin was resting quietly on Robert's shoulder as they drove north toward Parkston. She was relaxed now, sedated with a mild pain killer.

* * *

It was dusk when Robert stopped in the Taylors' farmyard. As Erin stepped from the car, she had bandages on each hand and grass stains on her shirt and the knees of her jeans. Relived their granddaughter was back home again, Bert and Florence hurried down the porch steps to greet her.

"Oh, Erin, we were so worried. I was beside myself thinking about you taken by those killers," Gram said. She used the corner of her apron to wipe away the tears.

"Well, it's over, and I really am all right," Erin said, trying her best to sound brave. The tired look on her face and weak tone of her voice told them she was exhausted.

"You do look weary, dear. Can I fix you some hot soup?" Gram asked. She held tight onto her granddaughter's arm as if she might lose her again.

"Thanks. I had a sandwich at the hospital."

"Can I get something for you, Robert?" Gram asked

"Thanks for the offer, Mrs. Taylor. I need to be going."

Erin didn't like the thought of Robert's leaving, but he told her to get a good night's rest. He would call her in the morning.

"I will if you promise to come for breakfast instead of calling," she bargained.

"It's a promise," he told her and kissed Erin's cheek. Even in the dim light, he could see the grateful look in her eyes.

Robert waved from his cruiser as it circled the farmyard to leave. Bert was sure he saw two bullet holes in the driver's side door. He was not about to mention them to his wife.

* * *

The hot shower felt wonderful as it splashed over Erin's tired aching body. When the bandages on her hands became soaked, she removed them and carefully washed her scraped knuckles.

Slipping into bed, Erin was asleep in seconds. She never felt the gentle kiss on her forehead as Gram turned out the light and closed her door.

* * *

24

When Erin woke the next morning, she wondered if what had happened yesterday was real. With her eyes barely open, she touched the place behind her ear where she had been hit. There was a slight bump and the spot was still tender, but the ache in her head was gone. She recalled that frantic moment when Robert, his revolver poised, had recognized her subtle gesture, signaling she was about to break away from Mann. That connection between them and their combined actions had probably saved her life and maybe his.

Hearing the sound of voices from downstairs, she turned to the clock on her nightstand. It was almost 8:30. She had been asleep for nearly ten hours.

When Erin entered the kitchen in her pajamas and robe, it surprised her to see Robert at the table with Bert and Florence. She had forgotten about his promise to come for breakfast.

"You're looking rested this morning," Robert commented, as he stood to pull out an empty chair.

"Thanks. I'm feeling much better." Her voice still sounded a little raspy.

"I have some interesting news," Robert said. "Yesterday I put in a call for Ted Gilbert. He called back last evening to leave a message saying the FBI has identified Lawrence as one Ernst Lieberman, a German national."

"I'll be darned!" Bert said. "He claimed he was Swiss."

"Gilbert said army intelligence uncovered he had been working for the Nazis as part of a secret project to flood the U.S. and Britain with bogus money. The FBI is still trying to figure out how the Chicago mob became involved."

"You mean this is all tied in to a Nazi war plot?" Erin said.

"Yes, it's quite a story, and you are the person of the moment." Robert said smiling. "By the way, Gilbert said to tell you thanks for all your help and hopes you're feeling better."

"Looks like our granddaughter is a hero!" exclaimed Bert.

"We already had a wonderful granddaughter before all of this crazy nonsense," Gram countered.

"Hey, I'm just glad it's over," Erin said. "There's been enough excitement for one vacation."

"Well, I can't be sittin' around here all morning," said Bert. "You young people have some breakfast, and I'll see you later." He downed the last of his coffee and headed out the back door for his garage office.

Robert said he needed to get back to town, and Erin walked him to the porch. He said he would like to fix a quiet dinner at his place the following evening if she felt up to it.

"I'll be fine, so let's just plan on it," she answered and kissed him goodbye.

Later in the day, Erin called her mother, to let her know what had happened, but she played down the details.

* * *

25

On Thursday night, Robert and Erin were in his kitchen having a cocktail before dinner. When she raised the glass to take a sip, he could see there were still small scrapes on her knuckles

"How are your hands?" he asked.

"Not bad. They don't hurt. Just a little stiff," she answered.

"Here's something you might find interesting," Robert said. He unfolded a current copy of the *Des Moines Register* and laid it next to her on the counter.

Erin put down her drink and picked up the paper. Her eyes moved to a bold lead half way down the front page. "LADY ATTORNEY FOILS COUNTERFEITERS!"

Robert studied her as she began reading the Associated Press article.

"A prominent Detroit attorney, Miss Erin Elizabeth Hays, has been quietly working with the FBI, and recently fingered a Chicago mobster as the killer of a German immigrant, Ernst Liebermann. A source at Army intelligence reported Liebermann had been an expert engraver working for the Nazis in a plot to flood the U.S. with fake bills. Liebermann had somehow managed to conceal a stolen pair of counterfeit plates when he migrated to the US near the end of the war. He had changed his name to Edward Lawrence and purchased a remote farm near Parkston, Iowa.

After Miss Hays uncovered the hidden plates, Liebermann's alleged killer and a mob associate kidnapped the young lawyer in a futile effort to make a deal for the plates. She and a second hostage were freed when

police gunned down both mobsters in a dramatic shootout at a motel near the town of Cherokee."

"I can't believe it!" Erin exclaimed.

"What's wrong?" Robert asked. "It seemed accurate to me."

"It reads as if I'm some big time attorney working undercover with the FBI to break up some mobster plot!"

"Erin, you know the papers try to make everything sound exciting," he said. "Besides, what they reported is accurate. It just appears sensational."

"Well, maybe this will finally be the end of everything. I wonder if this made the papers in Detroit," Erin said. She folded the *Register* and placed it back on the counter.

When dinner was ready, they agreed not to talk any more about the news story or what had happened on Tuesday. After a time, the question of when Erin would be leaving for Detroit entered their conversation.

"What are your plans?" Robert asked casually.

"You mean about leaving?"

"Yes."

"In a couple of days, I guess."

"So soon?" he asked.

"I'd better get back before they give my boring research work to some new attorney and realize they really don't need me," she said. Suddenly she was aware that tomorrow it would be nearly three weeks since the meeting with her uncle. In all the excitement, she had not given any serious thought to her future career at the firm.

After they had finished dinner, she complimented him on his great hamburgers and potato salad, *This man is a better cook than I am,* she thought. They cleared the table, and Erin washed dishes while Robert was outside putting away his grill.

"It's a lovely evening," she said as he returned. "Let's have our coffee on the front porch."

Outside, they sat quietly talking on the glider. They watched the sky slowly change color as dusk slipped into night. Fireflies danced above the lawn, while a chorus of male crickets filled the air with their raspy calls hoping to attract a mate. In a nearby tree, an owl hooted its low, somber cry.

When a cool breeze rustled the bushes around the porch, Erin shivered, hugging her shoulders, covered only by the narrow straps of her summer dress. Robert offered to get her a jacket and went inside.

Reaching the hall closet, he turned and found her behind him. "I don't think I thanked you properly for saving my life," she said.

"It isn't…"

Before he could finish, Erin placed both hands on each side of his face and kissed him. "Thank you," she said softly.

When he pulled her into his arms he could feel the coolness on her skin.

"Would you like my the jacket? It should keep you warm."

"I think it would be even warmer in your bed," she whispered. Erin took his hand and lead him toward the stairs. He followed without saying a word.

That night, they made love with the eagerness of a first time. Then, a while later, again, slower with tenderness. Afterward, lying nestled in his arms, she fell into a blissful sleep.

When Erin woke, the clock on the nightstand glowed dimly in the dark. It was 1:15a.m. She turned to face Robert. "Are you asleep?"

"Not really. Just dozing. Are you okay?"

"I'm fine," she whispered back. "I never mention to Gram about being this late. If I don't get back soon, she may be knocking at your door after the events of the last few days." Quickly slipping out of bed Erin said, "Don't get up, just remember my being there beside you."

Before he could protest, she was busy dressing. Erin kissed him goodnight, and holding her shoes, she disappeared into the hall.

Robert listened to the muted sound of the Buick as it backed from his drive to head for the highway. For the first time that night, he fell asleep. There was a faint smile on his lips where she had kissed him.

* * *

26

Early on Friday, Erin called Illinois Central Reservations and secured a berth on the Hawkeye for Saturday afternoon. Then she called her office in Detroit, to let Diane know she would be back to work on Monday. Her secretary was excited over the news story about Erin in the *Detroit Free Press*. Erin downplayed her involvement, but it didn't dampen the secretary's enthusiasm. Finally, Erin called Robert, saying it was her turn to buy *his* dinner, and asked if he would select a place and pick her up at seven.

Robert sounded pleased at the invitation, so soon after last night. He said he would take care of everything.

* * *

In the afternoon, Erin went to the garage office to chat with her grandfather. She told him about her plans to leave the next day and asked if he and Gram would drive her to the station in Cherokee.

"Sure, we'll be glad to," he replied, "though we hate to see you leave so soon."

Borrowing the Buick, she drove into Parkston and parked in front of the drugstore just as Joe Butler was returning from an errand across the square. He stopped at his office steps and called to her.

"Erin, could I see you for a few minutes?"

"Sure. What is it?" she asked.

"I would like to talk."

Erin said she was in no hurry and followed his slow climb up the stairs into the reception area.

"Well, look who's here!" Bertha exclaimed as they entered. "That was some ordeal you went through!"

"Yes, we were so relived to hear you came though it all right," Joe said.

"You must have been frightened out of your wits!" Bertha added.

"I had my moments," Erin answered.

Joe told Bertha they would be in his office and asked her to hold any calls. After the old attorney had ushered Erin down the hall to his private office, he quietly closed the door and motioned Erin to one of the large chairs facing his desk. Taking a seat in the one opposite her, he paused, collecting his thoughts.

"I talked to Bert just a while ago, and when he said you were leaving, I wanted to discuss something before you return to Michigan."

"What's on your mind?"

"Erin, I've practiced law here in Parkston for more than fifty years, but time is catching up with me. I need someone younger to step in and help with the growing workload. As we talked about at dinner last Sunday, there is so much I would like to tackle, but this old body just doesn't have the stamina any more."

"I understand," Erin nodded, suspecting why he was confiding this to her.

"A bright young person like yourself could be a real asset to the people in this area. I would like to see you stay in Parkston and help with my practice."

"Joe, I..."

"Please, let me finish. I would like to offer you a position. It would be a full partnership. We would start right off sharing the profits fifty-fifty. In time that would change in your favor until I retire. Then the practice would be yours."

"Joe, I'm flattered at your generous offer." She hesitated, not sure how to say no without offending him.

Joe continued. "Why don't you let me write up a partnership summary and send it to you in Detroit? You can give me an answer after you've had time to look over the details."

Erin felt relieved. It would give her time to turn him down with as little disappointment as possible.

"All right," she said. "Send me your proposal. I can't promise you anything, but I'll give it every consideration and let you know."

"Wonderful!" he responded, then rose to his feet, offered her a cordial handshake and wished her a good trip home.

Stopping at the drugstore, she bought some breath mints and a magazine to read on the train. On the way back to the farm, she thought about Joe's offer. She hoped it was right, letting him send her a proposal. She disliked the thought of rejecting it, but she owed him the courtesy of a considerate response.

* * *

That evening Erin was in her bedroom when she heard a car stopping out back. Making a quick check in the mirror, she headed for the stairs.

As Erin breezed into the kitchen, her grandfather looked up from his place at the table. "Have a good time tonight!" Bert beamed at his granddaughter.

"Thanks, Gramps! *I spent long enough figuring out what to wear,* she thought. Erin had on her beige linen slacks but a different blouse than she wore on their first date. She was running out of options with her limited wardrobe.

Giving Gram a kiss on the cheek, she dashed out the door before Robert had made it to the porch steps.

"Lovely as ever." He grinned holding the door to his Oldsmobile while she slid onto the passenger side.

"It has been a long time since a woman invited me to dinner," he said.

"Oh, when was that?" she teased.

"Now that you ask, probably never."

They both laughed, and Erin tried not to think about this being their last night together.

"Where are we going?" she asked.

"Some place I hope you'll like," he answered. They reached the highway and headed north.

* * *

Thirty minutes later, they were in downtown Spencer. Robert pulled the Oldsmobile into a parking lot next to a stucco building. There was a hand-painted sign on the wall saying "Parking for Tulipano Nero. The Finest in Northern Italian Cuisine."

Inside, the Florentine style décor greeted them with soft lighting. The sound of an Italian melody flowed through the room. When the maitre d' had seated them in a cozy booth with fresh flowers and a white tablecloth, Erin told Robert it was perfect. She was glad they were away from Parkston for the evening, just the two of them, out of O'Brien County, away from the possibility of a call for unexpected duties.

There was, however, a tentative edge to Erin's enjoyment. She still hadn't told Robert about her plan to leave for Michigan the next afternoon.

When dinner was over, they danced with other couples on the restaurant's smooth wooden floor. The touch of his body and his clean masculine aroma were especially stirring to Erin as they moved to the music's easy refrain.

After they had shared a dish of spumoni with their coffee, Erin excused herself for a trip to the ladies room. Stopping their waiter, she quietly settled the bill.

When they were ready to leave, Robert signaled for the check.

The response was, "There is no check, sir."

Robert turned to Erin. He started to protest.

She raised a finger to his lips. "It's my turn, Mr. Thomas," she said, with a smile.

On the ride home, sitting close to Robert, Erin found some music on the radio and hummed along.

As they neared Parkston, he asked, "Would you like to stop by my place for a nightcap or some coffee?"

"I was just about to invite myself," she said, squeezing his arm. Since the incident at the motel, the nearness of him gave her a warm secure feeling.

In the kitchen Erin pulled him close and kissed him. While Robert held her, Erin told him she was leaving the next afternoon for Detroit. He didn't answer, just looked into her eyes and returned the kiss. Deep in her heart Erin knew she didn't want to leave.

This time he led the way upstairs to his bed.

After they made love and he was holding her close, she wondered if they would ever be together like this again.

* * *

27

After breakfast on Saturday morning, Erin wanted to say good-bye to Rolf before leaving. She borrowed her grandparents' Buick and drove to the Lawrence farm.

Erin was no sooner in the lane when Rolf appeared and followed along beside her car. When she stopped in the farmyard, he sat outside the car door and barked as if calling her out to play. When she stepped from the car, he nuzzled her hand, then ran ahead barking. It pleased Erin that Gramps was considering moving the big dog over to their farm.

With Rolf at her side, she walked around the house. She stopped for a moment at the lilac bushes. Peering through the branches, she could see a warning notice posted above the outside cellar entrance. As Erin walked on, she felt strangely calm about what had happened here only a few days ago.

Later, standing at the car, Erin scratched Rolf behind the ears and told him good-bye. He cocked his head and gave her a puzzled look.

* * *

Late that afternoon, Erin was standing between her grandparents at the Cherokee Station. When the eastbound Hawkeye finally came to a stop, she hugged each of them in a tearful departure and climbed aboard her waiting train.

As the Hawkeye moved eastward, Erin stared out the window. She watched one vast field of green merge into the next. Then she began to leaf through the magazine purchased at the drugstore in Parkston.

"Nice to see you again, Miss Hays." It was Adrian Wills the porter.

"Thank you, Adrian. It's good to see you, too."

"If you'll buzz me when you go to the dining car for dinner, I'll make up your berth for the night."

"Thanks. I will," she answered. "The coach doesn't look very full today," Erin commented.

"No, ma'am. We'll pick up a few more passengers at Fort Dodge and some at Waterloo, but it will be a light trip."

"What about the private compartment?"

"It won't be occupied tonight," he answered.

It was welcome news.

Sometime later when Erin returned from a quiet dinner in the dining car, her berth was ready. Down the row, she could see some of the heavy curtains were missing at unoccupied spaces. The only sound was the low rumble of the rapidly moving train.

Erin grabbed her overnight case and headed for the women's lounge. Passing the closed door to the private compartment, she tried to dismiss the haunting vision of a lifeless body inside.

Back in her berth, Erin turned out the light and fell asleep thinking about Robert. She never heard the train's mournful whistle sounding its warnings while speeding into the night.

* * *

It was late Sunday afternoon when Erin arrived by taxi at her townhouse. Tired from the long trip and change of trains in Chicago, she left her unpacking for later. In the bathroom she filled the tub with hot water and squeezed in some jasmine scented bath salts and relaxed in the fragrant water until it began to lose its warmth. After her bath, Erin toweled off and put on a fresh pair of shorts, a clean blouse, and tennis shoes.

Hungry, she searched the kitchen cupboard and found a can of tuna. In the top freezer section of the refrigerator, there was half a loaf of frozen bread. *Not exactly the ingredients for fine dining,* she thought. *I've got to run to the store before they close.*

In her car on the way to a local grocery, Erin made a mental note to call her grandparents and Robert to let them know she had arrived safely.

Erin decided it would be smart to run her car for a while. She dropped off the groceries, downed a quick sandwich, then drove to Belle Isle Park. She stopped at the southern end of the park where Lake Saint Clair flows to the Detroit River.

As the western sun dipped low over the city skyline, she fed a flock of ducks the bread from her refrigerator. A pair of Trumpeter swans joined the feeding. Erin tried to remember if swans mated for life.

* * *

28

Diane Johnson was talking with the receptionist at Davis, Clark, Adams and Hays, when the elevator doors opened. "You're back!" She cried and rushed over to give her boss a welcome hug.

"Thanks for the friendly greeting. It's good to be back."

"From what I read about you in the paper, we're lucky to have you back!" Diane exclaimed, taking Erin's arm and escorting her to the firm's inner offices. "I'm dying to hear all about everything that happened."

"Maybe later. After being gone for three weeks, I need to concentrate on all the work that must be waiting. How are things at law school?" Erin asked, changing the subject.

"Good. We finished the semester on liability and contracts, and classes are over for the summer. In two months, my fall session is starting again."

"It must be hard with all the home work and attending classes three nights a week."

"Yes, but I'm looking forward to next spring and graduation," Diane said.

As they walked, Erin thought of all the case folders she had left behind.

"I hope my work table hasn't started collecting more pretrial work files."

"Nope, not one," Diane answered.

As they came to Erin's office, she noticed Diane's typewriter was covered. Inside Erin's small windowless workplace, everything except the furniture was clear. Even her personal items were gone.

"This isn't your office anymore. We moved!" Diane exclaimed.

"Why?" Erin asked, looking puzzled.

"Come on. I'll show you," Diane responded. As they walked by a row of secretaries, everyone they passed greeted Erin. All of them said how good it was to see her again. Finally, Diane stopped at Garrett Barton's door. "Here we are, *your* new office!

"Diane, what *is* going on?"

"Come in and sit down. I'll tell you what I know."

"This ought to be good," Erin said, taking a seat on a couch close to the door. She wanted to be ready to leave if Barton walked in.

"Remember when we talked on the phone, and I told you about Barton telling everyone he had the Beck case wrapped up, and later Frank Davis called him upstairs and chewed him out?"

"Yes, I remember."

"Well, last week Barton was late for a court date, and when he finally showed up, he was drunk. The judge had to call a recess. Later that day, the judge phoned Frank Davis, mad as the devil, and told him if that ever happened again he would hold both Barton *and the firm* in contempt!"

"Ouch!" Erin said.

"Ouch is right. The next day Davis fired Barton! A few days after the news story of your narrow escape and how you helped the FBI to break the case, Margaret came down from Mr. Hays' office and handed me a memo with instructions to move you into Barton's office.

For the first time, Erin recognized her personal items placed about the room. "But why this office?" she asked. "It's a partner's office and Barton had been in here for years."

"I've told you all I know. Some eyebrows have been raised about your move, but with Barton getting the boot, no one is saying much."

"What prompted all this, Diane?"

"If I knew I sure would tell you. All I know is, since the *Associated Press* article about your abduction by those mobsters, you've become a celebrity."

"I can't believe a newspaper article put me into a new office," Erin said.

"Mr. Hays wants to meet with you at ten-thirty this morning. I assume he'll fill in the details then. The appointment is on your desk calendar. I'll leave you alone and let you get oriented. Give me a buzz if you need anything."

"Thanks," Erin said, as Diane left.

Moving around the mahogany desk, she lowered herself into a high backed chair. This office was more than three times as big as her old one. Besides the couch and table with four chairs, there was a credenza behind the desk. A large window overlooked Michigan Avenue. Erin's head was filled with questions.

* * *

Later that morning, when Erin entered her uncle's office, he quickly rose and embraced her. "Erin! It's wonderful to see you safe and back with us again!"

"It's good to be here again, Uncle Max."

"Come, sit down and tell me about everything. I was so relieved hearing you managed to survive such a frightening ordeal."

For the next twenty minutes, Erin went over the events of the last three weeks. Maxwell listened attentively.

"It is a miracle you weren't seriously hurt or worse," he said when she had finished.

"There was a time at the motel when I wasn't sure if I would make it out alive," she said. Then, not wanting to belabor the event, she changed the subject.

"Uncle Max, why have I been moved into Barton's office?"

Maxwell's expression of concern changed to a smile as he answered. "A few days after the story about you became news, we started receiving calls. Many were from prospective clients inquiring about our firm and about you. We even had a call from an aircraft manufacturer in California who was interested in our representing them. The news about you has been a real benefit to the firm."

"Wonderful," Erin interrupted, "but what has that got to do with moving my office?"

"Do you know about Frank Davis letting Gilbert Barton go?"

"Yes."

"Well, after the publicity drew so much attention to the firm and portrayed you as a rising attorney, the senior partners felt it would be prudent for you to have a more suitable office. We also agreed you should be promoted to junior partner. It is effective starting today."

"I'm not sure what to say," Erin gasped.

"Don't tell me my niece is at a loss for words," he chuckled. "Take time to become oriented. By the way, if your new office isn't furnished the way you would like it, work up a proposal for redecorating, and I'll approve it. Meanwhile, you will report to Jim Clark on client development."

"Will I still be able to keep Diane as my secretary?"

"Sure, if that's what you want. Now that you're partner, she'll work exclusively for you."

"That's great. Can I put her in for a raise as a partner's secretary?"

"Sure," he said, smiling at her quick response to the new position.

"Thanks, Uncle Max."

When Erin left his office, her head was swimming with the morning's events.

* * *

The next day Erin had lunch in the firm's VIP dining room with her uncle, Jim Clark, and Alexander Laughton, the Chairman and President of Laughton Industries.

As a prospective client, Laughton, an eastern textile manufacturer, wanted to challenge a suit filed by the United Textile Workers Union. The union represented hundreds of Laughton's workers at five plants, most of them women. The plant manager at Laughton Industries in Burlington, Vermont, had fired six female workers, and the union claimed the firing had violated UTW's contract. The chairman said that, when he had read about Erin in the papers, he felt having a female attorney defending them against the union would present a more sympathetic approach to a jury. Eager to follow up with Laughton's suggestion, Clark mentioned Erin's trial record strongly favored the firm's clients. His comment impressed the silver-haired executive, but it embarrassed Erin. However, she let it pass and said nothing about Clark's embellishing her limited court experience.

When lunch was over, Laughton said he would discuss the matter with his board and would let the firm know about their decision.

* * *

Over the next two weeks, Erin was either at a business lunch or in meetings with Clark and prospective clients. One afternoon as she returned to her office after another long business lunch, Diane gave her a stack of messages. "The one on top is from some guy who claims to be a free-lance journalist and would like to write an article about your involvement with the FBI case in Iowa."

"Thanks, Diane. By the way, did your raise show up on your last check?"

"It sure did! Last weekend I took Billy out to a family restaurant and then a movie. With our tight finances, we haven't done that for a long time. I really appreciate your help with the increase."

"Hey, you earned it," Erin said, noting a trace of tears as Diane left.

During the evening, alone in her townhouse, Erin called her mother and talked for nearly an hour. Erin promised she would drive down to Kalamazoo just as soon as everything settled down at work.

Since her return, she had thought often about Robert who called her almost every weekend.

Terry Warner, her ex-fiancée, had called twice, insisting Erin should give him another chance. Saying she could longer trust him, she asked that he not call again as their relationship was over. He was the last person Erin wanted in her life right now.

* * *

One evening late in June, Erin returned home and found a notice in her mailbox for a registered letter. On Saturday morning, she stopped at the post office and signed for it. The return address showed it was from Joseph Butler's law office in Parkston, Iowa.

Later, at home, she opened the letter to find three typed pages spelling out the terms of an agreement. The proposal outlined what Joe had said that day in his office when he offered her a full partnership with a five-year phase-out giving Erin eventual control of the practice.

It took her a number of drafts to compose a proper response. She turned down his generous offer.

* * *

29

It was a hot, Sunday evening in July when Erin returned from spending the weekend with her mother in Kalamazoo. It had been their first visit together since she had returned from Iowa a month earlier.

Erin had been impressed with the progress on the new house. Construction was well on schedule, and the their wedding was set for the last Saturday in October. Erin was happy to see her mother excited and busy. Having so much on her mind helped to limit Martha's questions about the danger surrounding her daughter's abduction.

On the drive back to Detroit, Erin reflected that, during the visit, she had never mentioned anything about Robert. Since returning from Iowa, it was as if she had been trying to convince herself that their lives were too removed by both her career and the physical distance. After the past conflict with Erin's mother over her lack of marriage prospects, it seemed better to let the subject of Robert pass.

* * *

Monday morning found Erin in a boardroom meeting with the four senior partners. She wondered why she had been asked to attend. She didn't have to wait long for the answer.

Frank Davis, managing partner, was obviously pleased when he announced Laughton Industries had selected their firm to represent them against the United Textile Workers Union, and Erin would be the lead attorney.

"Well, what do you say, Miss Hays, are you up to the task?" The senior attorney's steady eyes challenged her.

"Yes, sir!" Erin answered doing her best to sound confident.

"Good! Get with Jim Clark and map out a strategy the staff can use to prepare our brief. When everyone is ready, set a meeting with the client." With an abrupt nod, he signaled that would be all.

As Erin left the meeting, she was thrilled. It was finally here! A high profile case with one of the firm's biggest clients, and she would have the opportunity to plead it in front of a jury.

Later, Erin was in her office studying a brief the UTW's lawyers had filed with the District Court in Detroit. They were asking for back pay and reinstatement of six female workers terminated over controversial illnesses at Laughton's Vermont plant, some thirteen months earlier. Laughton's management felt the case was crucial because their company's relationship with UTW had been deteriorating. The failure to win this suit, in their opinion, would have a significant psychological impact on future contract negotiations which covered all five of Laughton's plants, not just the one in Vermont.

Erin was busy reading when Diane knocked then entered. "Congratulations! I just heard the news about your leading the big trial with Laughton Industries."

It always amazed Erin at how fast news traveled through the firm's grapevine.

"I thought you might want to review your calendar."

"Thanks, Diane. Just leave it clear for now. I want to spend all my time on our trial strategy until we meet with the client."

"Sure. Just buzz whenever you need me," Diane said.

* * *

At home that evening, Erin had a call from her grandfather. He sadly related the news that Joe Butler had died the day before from a massive heart attack. Erin said how sorry she was and would wire some flowers in the morning. Bert added that he and Florence would be attending the funeral at the end of the week. He mentioned Joe would be buried beside his wife in the Parkston cemetery.

They didn't talk long, and afterward she thought about her letter to the old attorney turning down his partnership proposal.

* * *

A few weeks later, Erin returned home to find another registered letter notice in her mailbox. The next morning on her way to work, she stopped at the post office. The letter was from the law firm of Meeker and Roth in Sioux City, Iowa.

At work she opened the large envelope and found it contained a cover summary and a copy of Joe Butler's will. It stunned Erin when she read that she was the sole beneficiary of Joe's estate, which included the law practice and his home in Parkston.

Why in the world would he do this? she wondered, searching for some logical answer. Erin quickly read the pages comprising Butler's will. He had provided a comfortable retirement annuity for his longtime secretary, Bertha Milton, but otherwise left Erin everything. When she finished reading, Erin noticed a small personal stationery envelope inside the original one. It was sealed with tape, and on the front were the handwritten words: "*To be opened only by Erin Elizabeth Hays after my death.*" Inside was a short note, also handwritten:

> *My Dear Miss Hays,*
>
> *I'm sorry circumstances did not permit you to accept my offer of a partnership, which I fully understand. As you are reading this, I will have departed this world to be with my beloved wife. I have no living relatives; therefore, I am leaving my law practice and all real and personal property to you to do as you see fit. It is an old man's hope, and yes, a gamble that my doing this would induce you to bring your talent and energy to Parkston for the deserving people in our area. I pray that my action has not placed too much of an unfair burden on you. I wish you well.*
> *Warmest personal regards,*
>
> > *Joe*

Why, you old rascal, you put everything on the line with one last attempt to make me your partner even in death.

During the night Erin was had trouble sleeping. She hated the thought of how disappointed the old man would have been at her disposing of his law practice, yet she had no choice. Erin felt she must return to Parkston and settle his estate as quickly as possible.

Erin's firm had filed their brief with the court outlining Laughton's position. Since the initial hearing was not scheduled until early in September, she had time for a trip back to Iowa and could still prepare for trial on the long train ride.

After clearing her calendar for the third week in August, Erin called her grandparents and Robert to tell them she would be returning to Parkston. It was exciting when she heard the sound of Robert's voice. Erin knew part of her reason for the trip was to be with him again. She was pleased when he offered to meet her at the station in Cherokee. Erin couldn't know the impact this visit would have on their relationship.

* * *

30

Erin was alone in her office looking out at the bleak Detroit skyline. Dark clouds, heavy with moisture from the August heat, appeared ready to release their burden on the sweltering city. As she pondered the task of liquidating Joe Butler's estate, Erin hoped she was making the right decision. *Maybe I can find an attorney to take over his practice which might in part fulfill the old man's final wish.* Erin felt it could be difficult to find someone, but she had to try.

That night Erin called Robert to tell him that she was happy he had offered to meet her at the station and let him know what time she would be arriving. She also called her grandparents about her travel plans. Erin didn't give either of them a reason for returning so soon. She would tell them about Joe Butler's will in person. Finally, Erin called her mother, to let her know the reason she would be traveling back to Parkston.

* * *

Two days later, Erin was on the Hawkeye traveling by vast fields of corn, now more than six feet high. As she gazed out the window, she watched their tassels swaying in the early morning breeze. She smiled, remembering an event the previous evening. On the way to the women's lounge, Erin had nearly collided with a man stepping into the narrow hallway from the private compartment. Confronted by the elderly man in a dark suit and glasses, she gasped. Seeing the startled look on her face, the man had said he was sorry if he had frightened her. Quickly regaining her composure, Erin had told him she was fine. *I guess the vague image of Edward Lawrence is somehow still with me,* she thought.

When the conductor came through announcing the next town was Cherokee, Erin felt elated Robert would be coming to meet her. The train finally slowed to a stop. She moved through the vestibule and stepped down from the sleeping coach. There were a few people waiting for arriving passengers, but Robert was nowhere in sight. For a moment she paused, wondering if there had been a mix up about her arrival time. Thinking he might be inside, she walked toward the station entrance. All at once, the door of the waiting room opened, and there he was in his straw hat, khaki uniform and boots. The star-shaped badge on his shirt gleamed in the late August sun as he moved to meet her.

"Hi there, gorgeous," he said, sweeping her into his arms and kissing her. Robert took the overnight case dangling at her side and held her arm as they entered the station.

"Sorry for being late," he said. "There was an accident on the highway near Germantown. I had to take the call until one of my deputies could relieve me."

"Hey, you weren't late. The train just arrived," she said, happy to be with him again. Back inside the station, they sat together on a travel-worn bench waiting for her suitcase.

"How was the trip?" Robert asked.

"Good. No one murdered this time!"

"I'm glad," he said smiling.

Once her suitcase was off the train and in his cruiser, they were on their way to the Taylors' farm.

For a time, they drove in silence, as if neither of them was sure of what to say. Erin decided she needed to express something about the reason for her return. Yet she was reluctant to tell Robert about the old lawyer leaving her his estate, afraid it would lead to the suggestion that she take over his practice, although it wouldn't be like him to press the issue so soon after her arrival. Maybe the hesitation was because she didn't want to admit part of her wanted to consider staying.

Finally, knowing it would come out soon anyway, and not wanting him to hear it from someone else, she told him.

"It's about Joe Butler's estate," she said.

"I'm not sure what you're saying."

"The reason I've returned is Joe Butler left everything to me in his will. I have an appointment to meet with his attorneys in Sioux City later this afternoon"

Robert was surprised. "What are your plans for this unexpected windfall?"

"I'll try to find someone willing to take over his practice. Finally, my firm has made me a partner, and I'm scheduled as the lead in a major trial. It's what I've always wanted."

"I'm happy for you, Erin. I'm sure you'll do well," he answered, pleased now that she was here again, regardless of the reason.

When they turned off the highway to the county road, Robert asked when they might get together.

"I'm not sure what time I'll be back from Sioux City. Can we make it tomorrow night?"

"That would be great!" he said, as they turned into Taylors' lane.

Before they reached the farmyard, Erin saw Rolf coming from the barn. She was pleased to see that her grandfather had brought the shepherd over to their place.

* * *

Later in the day, Erin borrowed her grandparents' Buick and drove the sixty-eight miles to Sioux City.

"Good afternoon, may I help you?" asked the middle-aged woman seated behind a desk. She wore her hair pulled back into a tight bun, and her pinched features peered out from behind steel-rimmed glasses.

Erin guessed she was younger than her matronly appearance suggested. "I'm Erin Hays. I have an appointment with Mr. Meeker."

"Oh, yes," the woman responded. "Mr. Meeker said to show you to our conference room the minute you arrived. Please, follow me." She rose and led Erin down a hall to a well-furnished room much larger than the one in Joe's office.

"Can I bring you something to drink?" she asked.

"I'm fine for now, thanks."

"I'll let Mr. Meeker know you're here." As she turned to leave, a large man with a mop of thick dark hair above alert light blue eyes entered the room. He had a warm smile as he offered his hand to Erin.

"Hello, I'm Al Meeker. You must be Miss Hays. It's good to finally meet you! Please, have a seat," he said, pointing out a place at the conference table set with a yellow pad and a sharpened pencil.

"Would you like coffee or a soda?" he asked.

"No, thanks, I'm fine."

"Let Bob know Miss Hays is here Miss Rupert." The receptionist said she would and departed.

"Joe was a good friend. We go way back. He got the best of me in a civil suit some years ago, and we've been friends ever since."

The conference room door opened, and a portly man with a round ruddy face and sandy hair that matched his bushy mustache, entered the room. His image went with the western motif in the paintings covering two of the four walls. Although the table was blocking her view, Erin was sure he would be wearing cowboy boots.

"This is Bob Roth," Meeker said. The man shook hands with Erin and took a seat next to his partner.

"Well, we've been looking forward to meeting you, Miss Hays," Roth said. "That was some ordeal you went through with those Chicago gangsters!"

"The papers overplayed the whole incident, especially my part in the investigation," Erin responded.

"Nevertheless, we're delighted you traveled all this way to meet with us," Roth added. His wide friendly smile accentuated the fullness of his mustache.

Following a light knock on the door, a petite young woman entered the room. She held two file folders and a checkbook which she placed on the table in front of Meeker.

"This is Stacy, Miss Hays. She's our Girl Friday and keeps us old attorneys up to speed."

The youthful woman blushed slightly. "Is there anything else?" she asked.

"That's fine. Thank you, Stacy," Meeker said. She quietly left.

"Now, let's get down to business."

For the next hour, the two men took turns covering the details of Joe Butler's estate and the work they had done to speed his will though probate.

"As his executors," Meeker explained, nearing the end of the presentation, "we have worked with his secretary, Bertha Milton, who has been sending us the bills for his home and office, as well as deposits from clients for past services. We combined everything into one escrow account at a bank here in Sioux City. The checkbook in front of you is for that account. We employed a local firm to audit everything. Their report is in the file. They estimated the total value of his estate, including cash, to be just over fifty-five thousand dollars. Joe was specific about the confidentially of the will. Why he left his entire estate to you is something strictly between you and him."

"God rest his soul," Roth interjected.

"Are there any questions?" Meeker asked.

"No, everything appears in order," Erin replied.

"If you will just sign the release form, everything will be in your hands, and we wish you the best," Roth said.

Meeker nodded his agreement.

"Thank you both. I'm sure Joe would be happy with your execution of his will," Erin said as she prepared to leave.

"I have a question if you don't mind?" Roth said. "Do you plan to continue the practice?"

Erin hesitated. "With the commitment to my firm in Detroit it would be difficult to make such a change. I do plan to look for an attorney to take it over. If you have any leads, I would appreciate it."

"I'm sorry to hear you won't be staying, Miss Hays. You would have been a real addition to the bar here in Iowa," Meeker said.

"Thank you for the kind thought," she said.

* * *

During their evening meal, Erin told her grandparents the reason Joe Butler had left her his estate. He'd hoped she would stay in Parkston and assume his practice. It pleased Erin they respected her decision to continue as a partner with the firm in Detroit.

* * *

31

The next day, Erin parked her grandparents' Buick in front of the gray sandstone building that had been the center of Joe Butler's world for so many years. For a time, she sat quietly looking at the old attorney's office. It seemed strange knowing this barely familiar structure belonged to her. She was concerned that his longtime secretary and legal assistant could face the end of her employment after so many years of faithful service once Erin sold the practice.

"Good morning!" Bertha said. Her hazel eyes seemed to smile as she spoke.

It pleased Erin to find Bertha in such a pleasant mood. It would make the task ahead that much easier.

"Good morning," Erin responded.

"I heard you were back. I have been looking forward to seeing you again."

"You were expecting me?" Erin said.

"Yes, everything has been on hold since Joe passed away. Mr. Meeker's firm took care of the bills, but clients have been calling, and I just put them off until you arrived."

"How did you know I would be coming back?"

"My dear," Bertha looked at Erin with a knowing smile. "I've been with Joe for more than twenty years. During the weeks when he knew his health was failing, Joe told me about willing the practice to you and made me swear not to breathe a word about it until after he was gone. I cried like a baby at his funeral and for most of the week after. But you're here now, and I'm sure everything will be fine."

It relieved Erin that Bertha knew about the will, but it was obvious she assumed Erin was here to take over the practice.

"If you're ready, let me show you around the office. I'm sure you'll want to become familiar with the place." For the next few minutes, Bertha went over everything in the building. Besides the reception area and the conference room, there was another private office next to Joe's, which was also furnished with dark, heavy furniture. On the desk in an otherwise subdued room was a vase of bright summer flowers.

"This was to be your office when he offered you the partnership. I told him no woman would be comfortable in these drab furnishings, and he told me to perk it up with some flowers. A florist in Sheldon still delivers a fresh arrangement each week. I added one for his desk, not being sure which office you'd want to use."

"Joe was a good lawyer, but he wasn't much on decorating. Some of this furniture is so old it should be in a museum. He did insist on keeping the office clean and I mean spotless. We have a young man who comes in once a week and goes over everything including the floors and windows."

The last room down the hall was a combination of storage and a break area. There was a refrigerator, a coffee maker on the counter, and a small kitchen table with two chairs. A door that was the rear entrance opened to a concrete landing and steps leading down to three parking spaces. A 1940 Plymouth occupied one space; the other two were empty.

"That's my old dependable," Bertha said. "Joe's Chrysler remained behind the office gathering dust for a time after he died. I had the young cleaning man wash it and put it in the garage at Joe's house."

The mention of Joe's place reminded Erin she was also the owner of a home in Parkston.

Later, alone in Joe's office, Erin walked around looking at reference books on the shelves and lightly running her hands over his aging furniture. For a time, she resisted using the high-backed chair behind the desk, a silent reminder of the old man. Finally, she sat down, wondering what advice he must have given to hundreds of clients over the years. Her mind wandered to what counsel he might have passed on to her before she addressed the court at the up-coming Laughton trial.

On the desk, next to three sets of keys, she noticed a typed note from Bertha telling her they were for the office, the house and Joe's Chrysler.

Erin thought about all that was still ahead waiting for her decision. She remembered Joe's note saying he hoped leaving her his estate would not be too much of a burden. *Right now, Joe, it seems it is,* she thought. She had to tell Bertha she was not planning to stay.

When the town's siren signaled the noon hour, Erin left Joe's office and approached Bertha. "Would you like to go out for something to eat? Afterwards we might stop over to see the house?"

"That sounds fine," Bertha said.

They had lunch at a café on the square, then drove the four blocks to Joe's former home. Erin parked the Buick in the driveway of the large two-story brick house. It sat back from the street on an open, tree-shaded yard.

As they walked though the rooms, Erin felt she was a stranger in someone else's home.

"The same young man that cleans the office takes care of the house and yard," Bertha said. "It's ready to move in if you want. It might be more convenient staying here, rather than driving back and forth to your grandparent's farm."

"Bertha, we need to talk," Erin said as they entered the kitchen.

Bertha pulled out a vinyl padded chrome chair and lowered herself onto it.

With a serious look, Erin joined Bertha at the table. "I think you should know I'm not planning to stay in Parkston."

"Oh?"

"I'm not taking over the practice." She searched the older woman's face for her reaction.

"I'm not surprised," Bertha said. "I remember telling Joe when I typed the partnership offer there was little chance a bright young person like yourself would leave a big firm and come to a little town like Parkston. I can't say I blame you one bit."

"But, Bertha, if we can't find someone to take over the practice and become forced to liquidate, you'll be out of a job that you've had for years!"

"Erin, my dear, I'll be fifty-nine next April. When Joe died I was sad for the loss and will miss him dearly. Yet, since my husband passed away, I've yearned for the chance to leave Parkston and move to California.

I have a sister who lives in Santa Monica. She lost her husband a year after my Harold, and she's been after me to move out there and live with her. The last two winters I've taken my vacation time to visit her, and I love the climate. I'm sure you know Joe left me a comfortable retirement annuity, and my living expenses with my sister won't be much at all."

Erin felt relieved.

"Just tell me what you want me to do." Bertha continued, "I'll stay until the middle of November, then I would like to leave Parkston and make California my home."

* * *

That evening Erin was at Robert's house. She watched him across the table as they finished their dinner of fresh walleyed pike from a friend who had just returned after a Minnesota fishing trip.

"As always, your meal was great," Erin said.

"You've been lucky enough to be here at the times when my cooking efforts went well," he laughed. "A good many disasters have come out of my kitchen, believe me."

Erin was feeling good. She liked being with this self-possessed man who continually amazed her with his abilities. She could not deny the depth of her attraction to him, and it was sad to know she would be leaving again in a few short days. She was deep in thought as he was pouring their coffee.

"Hello there!" he said, a slight smile turning the corners of his mouth as he sat down again.

"I'm sorry. Just thinking."

"Anything you'd like to share?" he asked.

Wanting to be open with Robert, she related more of the details about Joe's partnership offer and the personal note explaining why he had left everything to her. "This would seem like a windfall," Erin said, "but it's becoming a difficult task. With my career at the firm finally beginning to work out the way I hoped, it would be foolish to give up what I have worked so hard for." Erin knew she was rationalizing to Robert although he hadn't challenged her decision to sell the practice.

Later, when their coffee was gone, Robert moved from his place at the kitchen table and drew Erin to her feet. As he pulled her into his arms, she gazed into his gray eyes. Drawing her close, he gently touched her lips with his and held her for the longest time. Finally she broke away and headed for the stairs to the second floor. Making love was much easier than trying to explain how she felt about him.

It was after midnight when Erin quietly slipped into bed at her grandparents' farm.

* * *

32

A light rain was falling as Erin parked behind the law office in Parkston. It was early, and Bertha's car was not there. Using her key to enter, Erin walked down the hall to Joe's office. A fresh vase of flowers was on the corner of his desk. Hanging the umbrella she had borrowed from Gram on a coat rack in the corner, Erin retraced her steps and returned to the storage room to make coffee.

As it began to perk, the rear door opened, and Bertha entered. "Good morning!" she said cheerfully.

Erin returned the greeting.

Later, as Erin was going over a recent bank statement, she noted a number of deposits. "What are all these credits?" she asked when Bertha came into her office.

"Some clients weren't always able to pay for his services right away, so Joe let them send whatever they could afford. Sometimes we'd have to wait until harvest in the fall when the farmers would sell their crops. I don't think we've ever had a bill that wasn't settled in time."

It amazed Erin until she remembered the financial statement Meeker and Roth had provided showing no outstanding bad debts.

"Miss Hays, we have a visitor, and I wondered if you would take a minute to see her? Mrs. Moorland. She and her husband were clients of Joe's."

"What's it about?"

"She wants to discuss the mortgage on their farm. Her husband was hurt in an accident last year, and they've fallen behind on the monthly payments."

"Doesn't she know about Joe?"

"Yes, but it seems she heard that you're here, and she wants to see you."

"I'm not sure if I can help, but please send her in."

When the woman entered, she appeared prematurely gray and much too thin. Her cotton print dress, faded from so many washings, hung loosely from delicate shoulders. Erin motioned her to a couch across from the desk and sat down at one end. The woman told Erin their mortgage company had sent a registered letter stating the Moorlands were six months behind with their payments. If they were not up-to-date in thirty days, the company would start foreclosure proceedings. "I've written their credit people and explained that, with our fall harvest, we'll have enough to become current, but they won't listen." There were tears of despair in the woman's eyes as she related her story.

"How long have you been paying on this mortgage?" Erin asked.

"More than sixteen years."

"Have you ever been late with the payments before this?"

"No. Since my husband's accident, we've had so many medical expenses and very limited insurance."

Erin paused, thinking. Finally she reached over and touched the woman's hand. "Don't be too concerned. With the promise of your harvest income, we should be able to make an equitable arrangement with them. If you would drop off a copy of your mortgage and the loan agreement, I'll contact them and see what they have to say."

"Oh, thank you, Miss Hays!" For the first time, there was an expression of hope on the woman's face.

That afternoon, after Mrs. Moorland had returned and left the papers with Bertha, Erin reviewed the loan contract and put in a call to the mortgage company. It was based in Des Moines. She asked to speak with a Mr. Howard Wright whose signature was on the mortgage as chief financial officer. When Mr. Wright's secretary came on the line, Erin identified herself as a partner with Davis, Clark, Adams & Hays in Detroit and said she would like to speak with Mr. Wright. In a short time he came on the line. Erin told him she was calling for her clients, the Moorlands, who received a foreclosure notice. She explained the client would be able to become current after the fall harvest. "I'm sure your company appreciates the Moorlands paying on time for many years, and that you would rather give them a chance to become current rather than have the expense of litigation over the issue," Erin said in a confident, professional voice.

"Not knowing the details of the matter, I will need to talk with our credit manager," Wright said. "I'll be glad to look into it and call you back if you'd give me the phone number of your firm."

Later that day, Diane called from Detroit with the message that a Mr. Wright had called asking if Erin Hays was a partner in the firm.

* * *

The next afternoon, Erin received a call from Wright. He said they had reviewed the Moorland's payment history and would be happy to send a letter giving them until the end of December to bring their payments current. Erin thanked him and said she would notify her client of their decision. When she hung up the phone, Erin smiled. *Wright must have wondered how a poor Iowa farm family had been able to retain the services of a large Detroit law firm.* With a couple of calls, she had been able to help this family prevent a possible foreclosure.

* * *

By Friday, Erin and Bertha had worked out the wording for a notice in various publications announcing the sale of Joe Butler's practice. There was still the matter of his house, but she decided to deal with that problem when they found a buyer for Joe's firm.

At noon, two days of rain had stopped, and Erin went out for lunch. When she returned, a woman and a young man were waiting to see her. Bertha introduced them as Mrs. Anderson and her son Tod. The Andersons had been past clients of Joe's. The woman appeared to be in her early forties; she was tall, broad shouldered, and neatly dressed. She spoke with a slight Swedish accent. Her son, a muscular young man in his late teens with neatly combed blond hair, looked shyly at his shoes as Erin shook their hands.

When the Andersons sat down in Erin's office, Mrs. Anderson told how her husband had lost his arm two years earlier when he tried to clear a jammed corn picker. He died because of substantial blood loss before they could get him to a hospital. She explained the financial strain his death had placed on their family.

"What is it you would like me to do?" Erin asked.

"I want to sue the equipment company that caused my husband's death!" the woman exclaimed.

It surprised Erin the woman would consider the challenge of taking a large corporation to court.

"Mrs. Anderson, what you are asking requires extensive research and a substantial amount of money to pay for what would most likely be a prolonged trial. It could take months or even years before reaching a settlement. There's a real possibility you would lose"

The woman remained determined. "I know there have been several families whose men suffered injuries working with Consolidator's equipment. Couldn't we all file a suit together?"

"Yes, it's called a *class action suit*," Erin explained.

"Have you had experience with such a lawsuit?" the woman asked.

"Yes. However, it took months before the trial ended, and, as I said, it was very costly."

"Please consider it, Miss Hays. We need someone like you who has the ability to make those big company people listen. I heard how you made the mortgage company back off when they threatened the Moorlands with foreclosure."

"I am so sorry about your loss, Mrs. Anderson, but I'm not taking over Mr. Butler's practice. I'll be leaving for Michigan tomorrow."

The woman looked disappointed, but she seemed undaunted. "I wish you would please consider it. We've talked to other lawyers, and they are reluctant to take on a large company like Consolidated Implement."

After the Andersons left, Erin sat quietly for a time. She understood why other lawyers had been reluctant to try such a suit. She recalled the Sunday dinner at her grandparents' farm when Joe had talked about that very situation.

It was nearly five o'clock in Detroit when Erin called her firm.

"When are you coming back?" Diane asked.

"I plan to be in on Monday."

"Well, hurry home. It's too quiet when you're gone, so I'm using the time to study. We have a big test coming up on liability."

"Mrs. Anderson would like to hear what you've learned on that subject!"

"Who is Mrs. Anderson?" Diane asked.

"Just thinking out loud. Would you let Jim Clark know I will be in on Monday?"

"I will. Have a good trip home."

It was nearly six o'clock when Robert called. He asked Erin if she would like to stop by his house after work for a drink.

"Sounds great," she replied."

* * *

After Erin finished her cocktail, Robert asked her to stay for supper. She agreed, and together they fixed western omelets.

"The omelet was just right. I eat too much when Gram is doing the cooking," Erin said. She rose from the table to pour some coffee.

"So, Bertha wants to leave Parkston and move to California?"

"Yes, that is one less concern. Now I'll have to wait and see what responses we get for an attorney to take over the practice."

"What will you do if you can't find someone?" Robert asked. "People in Parkston will miss not having someone here to help with their legal problems."

"I know. Already clients have been coming in asking for help. I guess I started something when I was able to help a family with their mortgage problem. News travels fast. Another family heard about it and wanted me to file a suit for them."

"Have you given any serious thought about taking over the practice yourself?"

Erin realized the conversation was heading in a direction she was not ready to address with Robert. "I'm about to begin my first big trial for the firm. The senior partners have put their faith in me, and I can't walk away from that obligation. Besides, it's the challenge I've worked so hard for."

Robert was silent for a minute before he said, "I don't want you to leave, Erin."

"Robert, I just told you why I can't stay."

"Erin, I know we can work this out. There is opportunity here to help people who need you. It may be selfish, but I don't want to lose you! I'm in love with you."

It was not what she wanted to hear. Not now, with all the things that were pulling on her. "Robert, it's not fair! It's too much to ask!"

He moved around the table and pulled Erin to her feet. He held her close, looking into a face that reflected her frustration and tried to explain, "It's not a matter of being fair. I've never met anyone like you, and I can't just let you go. There are many reasons that make sense for you to be here in Parkston!"

Erin was sorry she had let the conversation come to this point. A wave of disappointment washed over her. "Robert, stop it!" Erin pushed him away. "You're asking me to give up too much!" Now tears were spilling down her cheeks, and she could see the hurt on his face. *Why did you have to say you love me and complicate everything?*

"I'm not letting you leave without being honest about how I feel toward you, Erin." His voice was calm, "I felt strongly for you soon after that night we spent in Des Moines, but I was afraid of my feelings and unsure if I could love someone I hardly knew. If that creates a problem between us, then it's something we need to face together. Please, come into the living room. Let's sit down and discuss it; I know we can find a way through this."

"No! There's nothing to say! I care about you, Robert, but my life is in Michigan, and yours is here. Asking me to stay is out of the question."

Before he could respond, she abruptly brushed his lips, kissing him goodbye, and hurried out through the back door to the waiting Buick.

As she drove, Erin was angry with herself for the way she had responded to Robert. Deep in her heart, she knew she was in love with him. In the failing light, tears blurred her vision as the big sedan raced down the highway. Closing in on the county road turn-off, Erin hit the brakes and pulled hard on the steering wheel. The tires screamed as they grabbed the smooth surface of the concrete. When they hit loose gravel on the county road, stones sprayed toward a grassy ditch as the car spun around and came to a stop facing back toward the highway. Erin sobbed as she rested her head on the steering wheel. Salty tears flowed in tiny rivulets and dripped from the bridge of her nose.

The next afternoon, Bert and Florence drove her to the station in Cherokee.

* * *

"A jury consists of twelve persons chosen
to decide who has the better lawyer."
                    Robert Frost
                      1874 -1963

33

Erin and Jim Clark were in the firm's boardroom with the portly but immaculately dressed Alexander Laughton. Seated next to him was Louis Ralston, Laughton Industries' general counsel.

"We would like to review our approach to the textile workers' suit, then we can address any concerns either of you might have," Clark said, opening their meeting.

For the next two hours, Erin and Clark answered questions and explained what they had learned from pretrial investigations surrounding dismissal of the six women and how they thought Laughton Industries' case would stand up in court. When they finished, Alexander Laughton voiced his approval, while Ralston was more critical. "As you both know, the union has retained the services of Isaac Whitman, one of the country's top trial lawyers. With our labor contract coming up next year, it's imperative that we win this suit." The balding Scotsman's face flushed with emotion as he referred to future negotiations with the union.

"Louis," Laughton replied firmly, "We hired Clark's firm as one of the best, and I'm sure they will give us excellent representation against the union."

At noon, as Erin and the three men lunched in a nearby restaurant, Laughton quizzed Erin for most of the meal about events surrounding the kidnapping incident. It was obvious the attractive bright young lawyer impressed him. Ralston said little as he ate.

Later, alone with Clark in his office, Erin expressed her feeling that Ralston did not appear convinced about her position as the lead attorney.

"Forget Ralston," Clark assured her. "Just keep on your toes and go after Whitman. I agree with Chairman Laughton that your image with the jury will be a positive for us. If things get rough, I'll be right there at the table with you. Keep in mind that you have our firm's entire legal staff to draw on for support."

* * *

For a week, both sides labored over the voir dire process and finally settled on twelve jurors acceptable to both sides. Now the trial was ready to begin. The courtroom had filled early with spectators, including the press. Such a large audience was unusual for a civil case, but Detroit was a union-oriented town, and headquarters of the United Textile Workers. The presence of Isaac Whitman at trial always drew a crowd.

Erin, Jim Clark, and Bill Denning, the firm's attorney with a lengthy background in corporate law, took their places at the defense table. The union's lawyer, Whitman, and two associates, had already arrived and were in their chairs at the plaintiff's table.

As part of her pretrial work, Erin had studied the background on the famous Isaac Whitman. The press religiously followed the career of this seventy-year-old courtroom celebrity. He had represented the famous for more than thirty years. She had read his biography, published soon after Whitman had successfully won a lengthy highly publicized murder case involving one of Hollywood's brightest stars.

When Erin looked across the aisle at her opponent, the old man winked. His alert posture radiated an air of confidence. Erin nodded back with a tight-lipped smile. She was determined not to let him intimidate her.

Once everyone had taken their seats, the aging Judge Samuel Stone asked if there were any pretrial motions. Erin rose and faced the bench.

"Yes, Miss Hays, you have something to say?"

"Your honor, the defense asks that you dismiss the plaintiff's suit."

A murmur passed through the spectators, surprised at such a bold request.

"On what grounds, counselor?" Stone asked.

"We contend the plaintiff's suit is without merit, your honor." Standing before the judge, Erin felt her heart pounding. She was sure every eye in the room was on her. "The dismissal of the union employees by Laughton was based on a reasonable conclusion they were part of an already proven scheme to defraud the company when Laughton's accountant was prosecuted. Therefore, we contend their termination was in no way a violation of the contract as alleged by the United Textile Workers Union."

"You have a response Mr. Whitman?"

The old lawyer rose dramatically. He ran a hand through his long, bushy white hair. He shook his head in protest. "Your honor, the plaintiff strongly objects to Miss Hays' assertion. We intend to show the firing of these women was based on unsubstantiated allegations, and was therefore a flagrant act of intimidation by the management. Laughton was *never* able to prove any acts of wrongdoing by these unfortunate women."

"Your honor…" Erin began.

"Just a minute, Miss Hays. You made your motion. Now, if you don't mind, I'll make my ruling," Stone said in a stern, gravely voice. "It seems the reason we are here today is to give the union employees terminated by Laughton Industries their chance to be heard. Why don't we give them that opportunity? The motion is denied! Now, Mr. Whitman, let's move forward with your opening remarks while Miss Hays takes her seat again."

Erin felt a flush of embarrassment as she returned to the defense table.

"Don't let Stone upset you," Clark whispered to Erin. "The old goat loves to chide lawyers. We planned to come out strong and you did, so just stay in there."

For the next forty-five minutes, Whitman addressed the jury of eight women and four men with a passionate beginning. He paced back and forth, fiddling with a small gold chain that stretched across his vest. He promised to show Laughton Industries had violated their contract with the textile union and had been egregiously unfair to the women in question.

As Erin watched him, it was hard to believe the man was in his seventies. He was as lively as someone half his age. She watched his every move and found the senior lawyer impressive. *The man should have been on a stage,* she thought. *Maybe he is.*

When it was Erin's turn to take the floor for the defense, she felt as if butterflies were playing tag in her stomach. However, before long she began to relax and felt more comfortable as she addressed the jury. Erin stated the defense would show Laughton Industries had not been in violation of their union contract and had been well within their rights to terminate the employees in question since for weeks they had hidden their true condition while receiving pay for medical leave. She also challenged the union's motives as using this suit to strengthen their leverage in future contract negotiations with Laughton Industries.

When she finished, Whitman gave her a subtle smile and a nod of approval when she passed his table. Erin remembered reading that he would often compliment his opponents, deceiving them into thinking they were outperforming him. She had no such illusions.

It was after four o'clock when Judge Stone addressed the court. "It has been inspiring to hear from our learned scholars of the law, but due to the lateness of the day, we will adjourn until nine tomorrow morning." Stone rapped his gavel and the room erupted into a shuffling of chairs and unrestrained voices.

Late that night, Erin was in bed feeling restless and deep in thought. Could she stand up against this seasoned courtroom legend? Finally, she managed to fall into a troubled sleep.

* * *

The next day, as Erin climbed the courthouse steps, she looked her professional best. Her auburn hair had been carefully pulled into a tight bun, and under a well-tailored navy suit, she wore a simple white blouse. With briefcase in hand, she was composed as reporters firing questions blocked her way.

"Miss Hays, how does it feel coming up against the famous Isaac Whitman?" asked a young woman holding up a bulky microphone only inches from Erin's face.

"Do you feel you have a chance to win?" another reporter shouted before Erin could respond to the first question.

"Please! We have nothing to say for now," Erin answered. Hoping to hold off more questions, as she pushed through the crowd and entered the courthouse.

When Erin took her seat at the defense table, she noticed that her uncle Max and Louis Ralston were in the first row just behind the bar. Maxwell gave her an encouraging smile as Ralston acknowledged her with a slight nod.

Shortly, everyone stood as Judge Stone took his seat on the bench.

"Please, everyone be seated. It appears we are all here this morning, ready to impress the jury," said Stone with his usual dry sarcasm. "So, Mr. Whitman, why don't you start with the plaintiff's case?"

"Thank you, your honor." Whitman responded from his position at the table. "If it pleases the court, I would like to remain seated while I brief the jury on some specifics of the union's contract with Laughton Industries."

"Be my guest," Stone replied.

Whitman started reading aloud portions of the contract outlining the two weeks of full pay for supervisor excused illness and twelve weeks at half pay for the doctor-confirmed time away from work. Then, he rose from the table and began pacing back and forth in front of the jury box. "Laughton's personnel records document that none of the unfortunate employees were out longer than stipulated under the agreement, and the company's own doctor approved their medical leave! Yet, because of fraudulent action by Laughton's accountant, who was falsifying the payroll time sheets, the company callously fired these employees even though there had been nothing to show any connection between these employees and the accountant!"

"Objection!" Erin called out, rising from her seat. "Your honor, Mr. Whitman is straying from presenting evidence and is back making opening statements again, clearly trying to taint the jury's opinion of our client!"

"Yes, the court is aware of Mr. Whitman's flare for the dramatic," responded Stone. "The objection is sustained. In the future, Mr. Whitman, stick to the evidence and save the editorialized opinions for your closing."

"My apologies, your honor," Whitman pleaded, and called his first witness.

"Good work, Erin," Clark offered as she sat down. "This guy is going to play to the jury's emotions every chance he gets."

When Mrs. Inez Santiago took the stand and was sworn in, Whitman asked about her position at the textile plant and the nature of her illness at the time Laughton had fired her. In a strong Spanish accent, she related that she had worked in the warehouse labeling bolts of cloth for shipment and had sprained her back lifting the heavy materials.

"I out two months when I receive letter from company saying I no longer working there."

"And what hardship has this placed on you and your family?" Whitman questioned. When the woman answered, her dark eyes were moist with tears. "It is very hard because my husband has no work, and we have trouble with the many bills."

"How does this make you feel about Laughton Industries?" Whitman asked.

Before the witness could answer, Erin was on her feet again, "Objection!"

"Yes, Miss Hays?" asked the judge.

"How Mrs. Santiago feels about Laughton is prejudicial. I'm sure she would be unhappy about being terminated, regardless of the reason. Mr. Whitman is playing to the jury again."

"The objection is sustained. Please stay on the path with your questions, Mr. Whitman. Your obvious attempts to elicit sympathy from the jury are beginning to try my patience."

"I beg the court's pardon, your honor. I'm through with this witness."

The judge looked down at the defense table. "It's your turn, Miss Hays. Let's keep everything moving along!"

"I have only a few questions, your honor.

Mrs. Santiago, how long were you employed at the Laughton Plant before you were terminated?"

"I not sure," the woman said, confused. "Maybe three month."

"I would like to submit to the court personnel records of Mrs. Santiago's employment. The documents show at the time of her termination she had been working at the plant not quite eleven weeks. Tell the court why Laughton ended your employment."

"The company say I not sick and tell me I no longer work at plant!"

A rumble of voices passed through the crowd.

"Quiet!" Stone bellowed, banging down his gavel.

"How did your back feel at the time you received the letter from the company ending your employment?" Erin asked.

"I object your honor!" Again, Isaac Whitman was on his feet.

"And your reason, Mr. Whitman?"

"The witness cannot diagnose her own condition, and if Laughton's doctor approved her absence, then it is not a work violation of the union contract!"

"I agree, counselor. The objection is sustained."

At the judge's ruling, whispers again rippled through the spectators.

For the remainder of the morning, Whitman called the other five terminated employees to testify. He established that Laughton fired all the women before their sick leave time had expired, and that the company doctor had approved their absences.

The afternoon session bogged down when Whitman called to the stand a physician the union had hired. The doctor spent most of his time giving a detailed explanation of each woman's medical history and his opinion, which agreed with the company doctor's conclusions.

On her cross-examination, Erin established the union doctor had not physically examined any of the women but only reviewed their medical histories from the company doctor's files. The union's physician admitted that any physical examination of the women on his part would have been inconclusive. Nearly a year had passed between the time the women were terminated and the union requested his services as an expert witness.

For the next two days, Whitman paraded a list of previously terminated employees into court. He tried to show Laughton Industries was a ruthless and uncaring employer.

Erin was able to have much of their testimony stricken from the record as prejudicial, but she knew Whitman wasn't concerned because the jury had already heard their statements.

* * *

34

It was the third Monday in October when Erin entered the courtroom and took her place at the defense table. Every spectator seat behind the bar remained occupied.

The newspaper continued to comment on the case and, so far, their rhetoric appeared as favoring Isaac Whitman to win. The business editor of the *Detroit Free Press* did give Erin credit for performing well against Whitman.

The jury was in place, ready to hear from the defense. Erin called her first witness. "Your honor, I call Glendon Reynolds to the stand."

"Objection!" Whitman cried, rising quickly to his feet.

"We have hardly started the day, counselor. Didn't you sleep well last night?" the judge asked.

"Mr. Reynolds is on the plaintiff's witness list, your honor," Whitman protested.

"What bothers you about Miss Hays calling this witness, Mr. Whitman?"

"We were planning to call him only as necessary to establish the employment of the women in question for the record. Miss Hays is just probing in the dark by calling Mr. Reynolds. Questioning this witness will prove to be a complete waste of the court's time!"

"Excuse, me counselor, but I'll decide what is and is not a waste of the court's time! Sit down, and let's move along," the judge said, scowling at Whitman.

After the strapping Glendon Reynolds had been sworn in, Erin asked him about his employment.

"What is your position at the textile plant, Mr. Reynolds?"

"I'm the foreman of shipping and receiving."

"Does that include the warehouse?"

"Yes."

"Sounds like quite a responsibility. Don't you also represent the union as the plant's shop steward?"

"Yes."

"Doesn't that present a conflict of interest?" Erin asked.

"I don't see why. Laughton pays me as an hourly worker just like everyone in my department."

"But you also represent the union to those employees. Correct?"

"Objection!" Whitman called again. "Mr. Reynolds' position as foreman and union representative is irrelevant to the issues in this case."

"Mr. Whitman, are you planning to object to everything Miss Hays asks? Overruled!

You may continue, Miss Hays."

"Thank you, your honor," Erin said. "I have no more questions for this witness."

As she passed her opponent's table, Erin could detect Whitman's puzzlement at her calling on Reynolds's for such limited testimony.

"Who is your next witness, Miss Hays?" the judge asked.

"I would like to call Dr. Reginald Parker."

Dr. Parker ran a clinic in the town not far from Laughton's textile plant and was under contract to act as the company physician. He had been the doctor who approved the terminated women for medical leave.

For most of the afternoon, Erin kept Parker on the stand. She quizzed him about the six women's injuries and their medical history. During her pretrial deposition of the doctor, Erin hadn't been able to shake the feeling something was wrong but couldn't confirm her suspicions. Now that he was on the stand, she still had the same feeling but wasn't able to bring out any testimony from him that would help her case.

Late in the afternoon, on his cross-examination, Whitman asked the doctor why Laughton fired the women if he had approved them for medical leave.

"I must admit that I have no idea why," he answered.

At the doctor's response, a rumble of conversation filtered through the room. Judge Stone banged down his gavel and called for quiet.

"I have no more questions for this witness, your honor." Whitman said, apparently satisfied with the doctor's testimony.

"I think we've all had enough for today," remarked Judge Stone. "Court will convene again at nine-thirty tomorrow morning." He lowered his gavel for the last time, then headed for the door to his chambers.

* * *

When Erin returned to the Davis Building, it was after six, and the place was mostly deserted. As she entered her office, she noticed a large bouquet of burgundy roses in a crystal vase on her credenza. Erin picked up the small envelope beside the vase, slipped into the chair behind her desk and opened it. Inside, the card read:

"I hope the trial is going well. I miss you!
Love, Robert"

Her heart quickened as she remembered that last day at his house and the hurt expression on his face when she had rejected his declaration of love. She could still feel the touch of his lips and recalled her confused emotions as she had hurried away, nearly crashing the Taylors' car speeding recklessly down the highway. Erin's memory of that night filled her with regret. "I miss you too, Robert," she said softly.

"Did you say something?" Diane asked as she entered Erin's office.

"Just talking to myself," Erin answered. She dabbed at the corners of her eyes with tissue.

"Are you all right?"

"I'm fine. It's been a long day."

"The flowers came this afternoon; they're lovely. From your sheriff?"

"Yes."

"I was about to leave unless you need me," Diane said.

"No, I'm leaving soon myself."

"By the way, how did it go in court today?"

"It's hard to tell. I can't get a good feel of the jury. I seem to be doing okay. I'm not sure who is the biggest character, Stone or Whitman."

"Well, good luck tomorrow," Diane said.

* * *

On Tuesday, Erin was in court, but she was feeling anxious.

"Good morning. I see we're all looking alert today, so let's get right to it. Call your next witness, Miss Hays," said Judge Stone.

"I call Mrs. Penelope Tate to the stand."

Low currents of conversation went through the spectators as they looked around for a glimpse of this witness.

A conservatively dressed middle aged woman took the stand.

At the plaintiff's table, Whitman had his two associates looking through their papers to see if the defense had this person on their witness list.

"Mrs. Tate, you are Dr. Parker's assistant at his medical clinic. Correct?" Erin opened.

"Yes," the woman nervously answered.

"You are a registered nurse. Is that right?"

"Yes."

"How long have you worked with Dr. Parker?"

"It will be seven years in December."

"Do you recall Dr. Parker's examinations of the six women named in this suit?"

"I'm not sure what you are asking," the woman said, her voice so low that Erin asked her to repeat what she had said so the jury could hear.

"Your honor, I must object to this whole line of questioning." Whitman called out, his voice sounding exasperated. "We went through all the medical testimony with Dr. Parker yesterday. I can't see what his nurse can add."

"For once I'm in full accord with your objection, counselor. What do you hope to prove with this witness, Miss Hays?" Stone asked.

"If the court will just allow me to continue, I'm sure Mrs. Tate's testimony will prove to have a substantial bearing on the case," Erin responded.

"I'll overrule the plaintiff's objection for now," Judge Stone growled, "but there better be some relevance appearing very soon!"

"I appreciate the court's patience," Erin said. "Again, Mrs. Tate, do you recall Dr. Parker's examinations of the six women and his diagnosis relating to their medical histories?"

The witness appeared as if she hadn't heard the question and made no response.

"Answer the question, Mrs. Tate," directed Judge Stone.

"I'm not sure." Her voice was barely loud enough to be heard although the room was silent.

"I would remind you, Mrs. Tate," Erin said, "that you are under oath. Again, I ask whether you were aware of their medical conditions?"

"Objection!" said Whitman. "Miss Hays is intimidating her own witness!"

"Overruled. Answer the question Mrs. Tate," the judge said, impatiently.

"Yes, I recall the doctor's diagnoses of the women in question."

"Good," Erin said, "Now, do you agree with the extent of the injuries to the six terminated women documented in their medical records?"

"Objection," roared Whitman rising quickly from his seat at the table. "I don't know what Miss Hays is trying to prove. She continues to badger the witness about something that has already been confirmed by the union's physician and is now on the record."

"Your are out on a limb here, Miss Hays, and I am about to saw it off!" said Stone glaring down from the bench.

"Your honor, there are only two people who knew the true medial condition of the six former employees at the time of their termination, and Mrs. Tate is one of them." I am trying to show that Dr. Parker falsified those records as part of a blatant plan to defraud Laughton Industries, and I'm trying to prove Mrs. Tate knows about the falsification!"

At Erin's statement, Whitman was on his feet again. He shouted his objection as the spectators went into an uproar. Stone repeatedly banged his gavel for quiet. Finally calling a recess, He ordered all lawyers to his chambers.

As the six attorneys crowded into the Judge's private chambers, Whitman was complaining bitterly. "Your Honor, Miss Hays is attempting to pressure Parker's nurse into disputing the doctor's diagnoses. She is in no way qualified to do so. I take exception to her whole line of questioning toward this witness."

"Your honor," Erin pleaded, "I strongly suspected something was wrong when I deposed the doctor and nurse Tate, and I'm just trying to prove it. Please give me the opportunity to continue."

"Too bad, Miss Hays, you can suspect what you want, but I agree with Whitman, and I'm not allowing any further questing of Mrs. Tate. When we return, I will instruct the jury to disregard her testimony."

Erin looked to Jim Clark and associate Bill Denning for support, but they were silent. She felt something between disappointment with Clark and anger at the smug appearance of satisfaction on Whitman's face.

* * *

35

The following morning, Erin took a deep breath as Judge Stone instructed her to call the defense's next witness. Yesterday, she had hoped to keep Mrs. Tate on the stand. After the judge disallowed further questioning of Tate, it dashed Erin's hope of pressing the nurse into admitting something was wrong with the doctor's diagnosis. Now she had to pin everything on her last witness.

"I call Mr. Sylvester Lamar to the stand."

A tall, very thin young man strolled nonchalantly down the aisle. The baggy suit he wore hung limply on his narrow frame. It appeared as though he had lost a significant amount of weight. His slicked down raven hair glistened with an oily sheen in the room's bright lights. When he took the stand, the witness appeared surprisingly at ease.

After he was sworn in, Erin established that Lamar had been the plant accountant and was fired prior to the termination of the six women in question. Also, two months later he was prosecuted and sent to prison. He had been with Laughton for a little over five years. As a salaried employee, he had never been a member of the union.

"Why were you terminated from Laughton?" Erin asked.

"The company discovered I had been falsifying employee payroll records."

"Exactly what did you do?"

"When certain employees, usually newer hires with injuries, were out for more than two weeks, I would show them back on work status so their checks would be for full pay. To conceal my activities, I set up a dummy account and paid the employees on sick leave at half pay and deposited their full pay into that dummy account. It wasn't difficult. The plant accounting department paid local suppliers rather than the home office, and I *was* the accounting department!" Lamar seemed proud of his fraudulent scheming. "It was easy to cover what I was doing with more than two hundred employees working three shifts at the plant. There were always a number of workers on sick leave, and the money added up."

"How long did your deception go on?" Erin asked.

"About three years."

Again, Whitman was on his feet complaining. "Your honor, Mr. Lamar's intriguing story of white collar crime is touching, but previous testimony has shown the terminated employees were on medically approved leave and were never shown to have any part in Lamar's criminal activities. Miss Hays is simply panning for gold where there is none."

"Please bear with me, your honor. I can show a connection if you will allow me to continue," Erin pleaded.

"Get on with it then!"

"Mr. Lamar, how did Laughton find out about what you were doing?"

"Someone in corporate accounting suspected inconsistencies with employee payroll records and complained to management. They sent an auditor from the home office to investigate. Unfortunately, it didn't take long before he discovered I was doctoring the work records."

"What happened after the company terminated you, Mr. Lamar?" Erin inquired.

"I was prosecuted and sentenced to one year in the state pen but got out in seven months for being a good little inmate."

"Were any of the six women in on your scheme?"

"No."

"Then why were they fired?"

"I'm not sure. Maybe because they weren't really sick. I was in jail, awaiting trial at the time. I think the company assumed they were guilty, faking their illnesses, but Laughton didn't have enough evidence to prosecute, so the company just gave them the ax."

"Mr. Lamar, if these employees weren't really that ill, how were they able to continue on sick leave when they were required to check in with the doctor on regular intervals to be excused?"

"Simple. The Doc was paid to keep them on sick leave."

With Lamar's allegation of Dr. Parker's involvement, the spectators broke into a loud commotion.

Whitman was on his feet again as Stone continued to pound his gavel. "Quiet! or I'll have the room cleared!" he shouted.

When things settled down, Whitman apparently changed his mind and sat back down as Erin continued, again addressing Lamar. "Why would the doctor allow himself to become involved?"

"The doc has a gambling problem. He likes to play the ponies, and at the time things weren't going well at the track. He got himself in a financial situation, if you know what I mean."

"So, Mr. Lamar, you paid Doctor Parker to falsify the medical records?"

"Not me personally. I didn't want any connection with the Doc, so I took my cut and paid the balance to my partner. He paid off the doctor."

The courtroom was totally silent as everyone, including the judge and Whitman, were glued to the young man's testimony.

"Let's get back to your partner," Erin continued. "Just how did he fit into your scheme?"

"He punched the sick leave employees in and out each day as if they were at work. I needed the weekly time cards to accompany my phony reports which were sent to the payroll department in Boston."

"The records of your trial show you were the lone conspirator at the time of your prosecution. What about your accomplice?"

"When I was caught, we made a deal. He promised to pay me if I took the fall alone. I agreed. I was headed for prison anyway."

"Why are you telling all this now?"

"Because I did the time, and the son-of-a-bitch never came through as he promised!"

"Will you tell us who that person is? I remind you that you're under oath." Erin's butterflies were back again as everything depended on this last bit of Lamar's testimony.

"It was Mr. Big Shot, Reynolds."

"Do you mean, Glendon Reynolds, Laughton's warehouse foreman and UTW's union's steward Erin asked.

"Yes!"

With Lamar's indictment of Reynolds, a roar went up that rattled the court room windows. Above the din, Judge Stone repeatedly pounded his gavel. When the noise continued, he ordered the bailiffs to clear the room. Then he ordered the lawyers to his chambers.

As the attorneys stood by silently, Judge Stone was agitated. "If Lamar's testimony is correct, implicating Parker and Reynolds, then there is complicity on both sides of this case. In a moment, we will all go back in the court room while I call a recess until nine-thirty tomorrow morning. In the meantime, I'll decide whether to entertain motions from both sides or just declare a mistrial. I'm sure we have confused the jury to a point they wouldn't know how to vote," he said, red-faced with frustration.

* * *

Later in the day, when Erin returned to her office, there was a phone message from Joe Butler's secretary. When Erin returned the call, Bertha said her sister in California was quite ill. She wanted to leave Parkston as soon as possible. Erin explained she was at a critical point in her trial and she would call back before the end of the week with final instructions for disposing of Joe's property.

Erin was home folding laundry that evening when Jim Clark phoned telling her an aide had just called to let him know Judge Stone had been taken to the hospital for an emergency hernia operation. The aide said it was too soon to tell anything more about the judge's condition, but court proceedings for tomorrow were canceled.

* * *

The next afternoon, Clark came into Erin's office with the news that Stone had come through his operation just fine, but the trial would be postponed for at least two weeks. Clark asked her to work on a response if the judge did call for motions upon his return and added that until a new court date was set, there was little else they could do.

* * *

36

A number of unresolved issues continued to weigh heavily on Erin. Uppermost was her concern for the trial. This delay could be a blessing as it could provide more time to develop a motion before Judge Stone, including an opportunity to hone her final statement to the jury.

This delay would also allow her time to relax at her mother's wedding, scheduled for the following Saturday. She still had to deal with the disposition of Joe Butler's estate. There had been no serious responses from her ads about Joe's practice, and Erin felt it was time to give his office and house to a realtor.

Then there was Robert. She had not responded to his beautiful roses and tender note. Erin was feeling guilty for the way she had left Parkston without giving him a chance to discuss their relationship. Erin's foolish reaction that night continued to haunt her.

The following day she called Bertha saying to expect her in Parkston early next week.

* * *

On Saturday afternoon, Martha and Dr. Paul were married in the living room of their new home in Kalamazoo. It was a quiet ceremony limited to family and a few close friends. The reception that evening at the country club was a much grander affair. The ballroom had been converted into a wondrous autumn scene with huge bouquets of fall flowers everywhere. The silverware and china gleamed in the soft candle light, while a live orchestra played to a dance floor filled with carefree couples.

Sitting alone at the head table, Erin watched the happy guests as they flowed though the open French doors to enjoy an unseasonably warm evening this last weekend in October. It was a welcome break to lose herself for a while in the merriment and put aside everything that still lay ahead. Lost in thought, Erin wished Robert were there to share this special day. Her uncle returned to the table. "Your mother and her new husband have thrown quite a party for their friends," Maxwell said, setting down his drink and taking a seat beside Erin. He saw the faraway look in the eyes of his niece and was silent until she responded.

"Yes, they seem to be very happy."

"We haven't had a chance to talk. I wanted to let you know that you have handled yourself well against Isaac Whitman. I understand you impressed Frank Davis the day he came by to watch the proceedings. I'm sorry I wasn't in court when you questioned that Lamar fellow. Clark said, if the jury believes Lamar's testimony, you may have won the case for Laughton. Let's hope Judge Stone doesn't call a mistrial."

"Thanks for the compliment, Uncle Max. I'll be holding my breath until Stone returns and gives his ruling. I told Jim I would be working on a motion to continue the trial. If Judge Stone grants it, I feel confident the evidence will convince the jury to vote in favor of our client."

* * *

The next day area weather had turned crisp, signaling the approach of an early Michigan winter. Erin accompanied her mother and Dr. Paul to the Kalamazoo station. The newly married couple were taking a train to New York City for their honeymoon. An hour later, Erin would be catching her westbound Limited for Chicago.

When the couple's train arrived, it was an emotional moment between mother and daughter as they embraced. Erin also shared a hug with her new stepfather as she told them good-bye.

Alone on the cold platform, Erin feeling a chilly breeze, pulled up the collar of her coat as she watched their eastbound train disappear from view.

* * *

37

The Hawkeye's engine billowed black sooty smoke toward an ashen sky as Erin's train thundered into the station at Cherokee late Monday morning.

When she stepped onto the platform and greeted her grandparents, they were glad to see her again but seemed strangely subdued. Their mood matched the day's cold, dreary weather. On the drive home, Gram told Erin that Sven Larson had been killed at their farm in a machinery accident. Erin recalled the young Swedish farmhand and understood her grandparents' somber disposition.

As they continued north on highway 59, the gloom lifted slightly when Gram asked about the wedding. She said how sorry they were not being able to attend, saying everyone was working seven days a week to bring in their late harvest before more rain started again. When they turned into the farm's lane, Erin saw Rolf suddenly appear. She was happy to hear the familiar sound of his bark as he ran beside their car. When they stopped, he waited near the porch steps. His thick brown and black tail swished back and forth, welcoming their arrival.

"I'm not sure whether we adopted him or he adopted us. Anyway, he is part of the family now," Bert said, as the slightest hint of a smile crossed his face. It was the first glimmer of the buoyant grandfather she had left behind in August.

As soon as they entered the porch and the screen door closed behind them, the shepherd barked a final greeting before heading toward the barn.

Later, while Erin was settling herself in their guestroom, she could hear Gram bustling in the kitchen, busy feeding a table of field hands. The loud voices and moments of spontaneous laughter that usually accompanied their noon meal were missing. It was obvious they all mourned the loss of Sven.

Afterward, alone in the kitchen with her grandmother, Erin was finishing the last of a sandwich. She wondered what Gram did to make even cold chicken so delicious. Erin was that sure that if her grandmother had a restaurant in Detroit, patrons would wait in long lines for the taste of her cooking.

Later, Erin descended the porch steps for a walk. The crisp November weather began to show promise as the sun peeked out from behind steel gray clouds. Near the barn, Rolf was watching Sonny and a second man she didn't recognize as they worked on a large conveyor. When the shepherd noticed Erin, he bounded to her side and nuzzled her gloved hand.

"Hey boy, it's good to see you again," she said realizing she had missed the big dog's friendly greetings and his insatiable desire for affection.

The men stopped their work as Erin greeted Sonny and expressed how sorry she was about Sven. Sonny nodded, silently responding to her condolence before he introduced the second man. "This here is Lester Higgens. He's the repair man from our local farm equipment dealer."

"Nice to meet you, ma'am," Lester said, touching the bill of his cap.

"Thank you, Lester. Don't let me keep you from your work," Erin responded.

"No problem. I'm just about finished installing this new drive chain. It's a shame the other one broke and hit poor Sven. He must have been twenty feet away from what Sonny tells me."

"On equipment this new that chain shouldn't have broken!" Sonny said disgustedly.

"Was it unusual for this to happen?" Erin asked.

"It's not the first time one of these links has broken and the chain went flying," Lester said. He removed his cap and wiped drops of sweat from his brow. Dressed in heavy clothing, he was perspiring even in the cool air. "I had to repair one last year up near Sheldon where the chain flew off barely missing the guy running it. Two years ago the field rep from Consolidated Implement told us they were planning to use stronger links and install a guard to prevent the chain from flying off if it did break."

"Well let's hope they will add those improvements to the newer models," Erin said.

"I'll believe them when it happens," said the repairman. "We got two new '49 models in last week, and they hadn't made any alterations from the previous year."

"If it costs them money, they ain't in any hurry to improve anything!" added Sonny.

* * *

I'm so glad you made the trip back to Parkston," Bertha said as they sat in Joe's office that afternoon. "My sister is after me to come out as soon as possible. I'll feel so much better about leaving now you are here to settle everything."

Later in the day, Erin met with a realtor from Spencer and signed the contracts putting Joe's office and house up for sale.

When the realtor was gone, Bertha mentioned her own place. "I found someone to rent my house which will give me some extra income."

"That's great Bertha," Erin said. "I hope it doesn't turn out that I have to rent either of Joe's properties if they can't find a buyer."

When Bertha left for the day, Erin went through the bills and a few checks Bertha had ready for deposit. In the mail, she found an unopened letter with the word "PERSONAL" typed in bold letters on the envelope addressed to her at the office. The return address was from "The Farmers Action Committee."

> *Dear Miss Hays,*
>
> *I wanted you to know that we have formed an association to press forward in our hope of filing a suit as we discussed. Our goal is to raise enough money to support a prolonged trial against Consolidated Implement Company as the major supplier of dangerous equipment.*
>
> *We have found an ex-employee of CIC who was a design engineer with them for several years. He has indicated his*

willingness to testify against his former employer in court.
The committee is praying you will be the one to help us.
Sincerely,
Mrs. Martin Anderson,
Chairperson

As Erin put down the letter, she felt regret for disappointing so many in Parkston that believed in her. She was deep in thought when the phone rang.

"Hi," Robert said, his voice friendly but slightly hesitant. "I heard you just arrived this morning, but I wondered if there was a chance we could get together sometime?"

Erin knew it must have been difficult for him to call. "Yes, I know we need to talk," she said.

"What would you like to do?" he asked.

"I plan to stay with my grandparents this evening. They are feeling the loss of Sven Larson. Tomorrow night would be better. Maybe we could drive up to Sheldon to Tom's Steak House."

"Sounds good" he said. "Pick you up at six-thirty at the farm?"

"That would be fine. See you then," she said, gently replacing the receiver.

* * *

38

The next evening found Erin and Robert at Tom's seated in the front dining room. Being a week night the place was quieter and barely half-full.

After they had ordered their dinners and the waitress had brought their drinks, Robert raised his glass. "It's good to be with you again, Erin."

"It's nice to be with you, too," she answered. They were both as polite and formal as strangers on a first date.

"I'm surprised you came back so soon." His smile helped to soften the moment.

"I guess I would be less than honest, and maybe even fooling myself if I said the only reason for my return was to put Joe's property on the market. I'm sorry I ran off that night without giving either of us a chance to talk," she said.

"Is that the reason you didn't call or write?"

"I'm sure feeling guilty is part of it. The trial took up so much of my time, and I just blocked out everything else. I want you know I do care about you very much."

Before he could respond, the waitress brought their orders.

As they began to eat, Erin could see from the look on his face that her words had not been the ones he had wanted to hear.

"Please believe that I understand the logic of your decision, Erin. When I told you I loved you, I knew there was a risk, but I'm not going to press the issue and make things worse between us. Who knows where time will take us."

Erin felt relieved that he was declaring a truce over the issue between them.

After a long silence while they ate, Robert brightened. "I have some news that you might find interesting," he said.

"Yes?"

"I was in Des Moines last week meeting with the Governor. Did you happen to read about Walter Sullivan's death a few weeks ago?"

"No, I haven't," she answered. "Who is he?"

"Walter was Iowa's congressional representative from our northwest district. He died of a massive stroke two weeks ago on his trip home from Washington. When I met with the Governor, he asked if I would fill the balance of the congressman's term."

"Robert, I don't know what to say! It's wonderful news! But, how...?

"When I came home from the war, the town went overboard with their welcome."

"Yes, my grandparents had mentioned the celebration."

"Well, it's when we first met. After my successful election to sheriff, he requested that I accompany him when he stumped through the district on his re-election campaign last fall. For the first time, he carried the surrounding counties by a wide margin. He seemed to feel my presence was part of the reason."

"Don't keep me in suspense. What did you tell him?"

"I told him I would like some time to decide. It's a tremendous leap from county sheriff to the United States House of Representatives."

"Oh, Robert, just think what it could mean! It's the opportunity of a lifetime!"

Excitement about his possible appointment filled their conversation for the rest of the meal.

On the drive back to the farm, Erin promised to spend another evening with him before returning to Detroit.

* * *

It was Thursday when Erin told her grandparents she had closed the law office for good, and that Robert would be driving her to the station the next afternoon. That evening Erin and Robert went to Spencer for dinner at the little Italian restaurant.

They both worked hard to make their evening as pleasant as the first time, but it was difficult. Their relationship could well be over. At the farm, when they kissed goodnight and held each other, neither one moved to let go. Finally, Erin broke away and ran up the back steps. On the porch she stopped and waved. There were tears in her eyes as she watched him drive away.

The next afternoon at the Cherokee station, Erin kissed Robert good-bye for the last time. She barely noticed the biting cold wind as she ran to catch her departing train.

* * *

39

Erin was the first person to arrive at the Davis Building on Monday, the second week in November. She went through her mail and messages. Then she began reviewing her notes on the trial when Jim Clark entered her office.

"I had a call from Judge Stone's clerk, the judge is doing much better with his recovery from surgery and wants to hold court this Wednesday, just long enough to hear motions from both sides. If the judge agrees to continue the trial, I feel you have a good chance to convince the jury to decide for Laughton.

* * *

Wednesday morning, Judge Stone allowed only the lawyers and the stenographer in the courtroom when he addressed the union's attorney, "Mr. Whitman, do you have a motion?"

"Yes, your honor."

"Please continue."

Whitman took his time. He rose from his seat at the table to address the judge, "The plaintiff still contends Laughton fired the women named in our suit in violation of their contract with the union. Mr. Lamar's indictment of Laughton's foreman, Glendon Reynolds, is a separate issue from our suit. In Lamar's testimony, he stated the terminated employees were *not* part of his fraudulent actions against the company."

"Mr. Whitman," Judge Stone interrupted, "there is no jury present for your closing statement. It would be nice if I could hear something that sounded like a motion." Stone's voice was weaker than before his surgery, but the tone was still as caustic.

"Yes, your honor. The plaintiff asks that you disregard Mr. Lamar's testimony as irrelevant to the issue of our suit. We also ask that you conclude any further proceedings directing the jury to adjourn and determine the level of reparation for both the employees and UTW." Whitman knew this was a long shot, but it would save the judge from declaring a mistrial and prevent the court from having to retry the case.

"I'm sorry, Mr. Whitman, but Lamar's testimony isn't irrelevant. It places Mr. Reynolds, as the union's representative, in the center of the sick leave issue. So far, there has been no hard evidence to prove whether the terminated employees were medically unable to work at the time Laughton ended their employment. All we have are the doctor's records and his testimony, and now that has been challenged by Lamar's indictment of him. It's up to the jury to decide who and what to believe. Your motion is denied!"

When Whitman returned to his chair, he was not happy with the judge's ruling.

"Miss Hays, anything from the defense?"

"Yes, I move the court continues with the trial, and if your honor is so pleased, the defense has no more witnesses to call."

"Granted, We will begin with summations from both sides on Monday at nine." With a light rap of his gavel, Judge Stone ended the day's proceedings.

* * *

During the next two days, Erin worked to sharpen her closing for Monday. Diane had just left Erin's office, after giving her the final draft, when the phone rang. It was Maxwell's secretary, Margaret, letting Erin know Mr. Hays would like to see her at 4:00 p.m. in his office.

When Erin arrived, Maxwell and Jim Clark were seated at a conference table in her uncle's office. Both men rose to greet her as she entered.

"Please join us," Maxwell said pulling back a vacant chair. "I'm sorry I was only able to be in court a few times, but as I mentioned before, you handled yourself well against Whitman."

"Yes," Clark added, "we felt you did just fine, and I'm sure the judge's continuing the trial for summations will play in our favor."

"Thanks for your kind remarks. I'm looking forward to Monday," Erin said, wondering what the compliments were leading to.

"That's what we wanted to discuss with you," her uncle said.

"Yes?"

"So much is riding on the closing," Clark injected. "The outcome could ultimately cost our client a great deal if the jury goes against us."

"Yes, I know," Erin said. She was beginning to feel uneasy, noting the serious expressions clouding their faces.

"Erin," Maxwell said, "we feel you have presented yourself well. Unfortunately, Louis Ralston is worried about how the jury will vote."

"Ralston has been wringing his hands through the whole trial. When the jury decides in our client's favor, he can stop worrying," Erin said, annoyed at the mention of Laughton's general counsel.

"We agree," Maxwell continued, "but Ralston has convinced his chairman that a seasoned attorney should make the final summation, even against our objection the lead counsel should not be changed this late in the trial. Ralston insists that Jim here should present the closing."

Her uncle didn't say the word, but she knew Ralston wanted a *man* to step in and save the day. There it was, the old male dominance monster coming out of the closet at the final hour. Erin struggled to keep her composure as she recalled Clark's words of support when the trial had begun, then his failure to back her when Judge Stone had thrown out nurse Tate's testimony. Unable to contain her feelings, she lashed out, "This has been *my* case from the beginning!" Her voice rising in anger. "I bring the trial down to the conclusion and you take it away from me?" Her fiery green eyes were moist with emotion, but Erin was not about to let them see any tears which could confirm even the slightest doubts they, or anyone else might have about her ability to close and win the case.

"I have every confidence in you, Erin," Clark said, trying to calm her. "But you know who pays the bills. Laughton is the client. He has the final say."

"They may pay the bills, but it doesn't make them right! You could have stood your ground, but you caved in when money got in the way!"

The two senior partners were silent as Erin rose from the table and stormed out of the meeting.

Later, in her office, Erin calmed down. She wondered if any junior partner who had told off the management was still around. She also wondered why Frank Davis hadn't been at the meeting. The firm's managing partner who had given her the lead in the case had been nowhere in sight. He left it up to others to do the dirty work.

When Judge Stone convened the trial on Monday, Erin sat quietly at the defense table. Jim Clark gave the closing she had prepared.

The jury was out for two days with their deliberations. When they returned, finding in favor of Laughton Industries, Erin was not surprised. She thought it ironic this trial was held in the same courtroom where this spring she had won the case for Allen Beck.

* * *

40

At the end of January, Erin received her partner's share for the previous year and a bonus for her lead in the Laughton trial. Between the two, Erin's total awards equaled nearly two years' salary. The money did little to sooth the humiliation of being replaced.

* * *

It was February when Diane came into Erin's office with the latest mail delivery.

"How would you like to go out for lunch?" Erin asked. "My treat."

"Sounds like a great idea, especially the part about you buying." Diane answered.

"Good! Call that fancy restaurant, the one next door to the Book Cadillac Hotel, and get us a reservation."

Shortly after twelve o'clock, Erin and Diane were at a quiet corner table looking over their menus when the waiter brought two champagne cocktails. They gave him their food orders, then Erin raised her glass, "Well here's to us. All the best in the coming year!"

"I'll drink to that," Diane said. Her expression became more serious. "Erin, I don't mean to pry, but for some time you have seemed removed, as if your thoughts are somewhere else.

Erin sighed. "It seems too much of my life has not turned out the way I hoped it would."

"Sounds like man troubles could be part of it. Are you still in touch with your sheriff?"

"No, not since I returned from Iowa in November. I can't blame him, though. I was the one that pushed him away, and being the person Robert is, he respected my decision," Erin responded. "Most of my life everything seemed so easy, until I became a lawyer. I grew up in a fine home with great parents. Mother got on my case now and then, fretting about marriage, but she meant well."

"Tell me about mothers! Mine calls at least once a week wondering when I'm going to find a man to take care of Billy and me!" Diane exclaimed.

For the next hour they talked, had more wine with lunch, and Erin confided the disappointment with her career ambition to be a successful trial lawyer.

"Erin, I look at you in your fancy office and have a good idea of the salary you make, and it seems like a dream to me," Diane said, surprising Erin with her candor.

"Diane, money is not the issue with me. I guess I'm just tired of having to prove something to a world of men because I'm a woman."

Diane was well aware of Erin's frustration, especially the disappointment Erin had suffered at the end of the Laughton trial.

"I hate sounding like an ungrateful complainer," Erin said.

Let's talk about what's new with you Diane."

"Not much since my husband, Cal, died in the war. You know it's been a challenge raising Billy alone. Between work and night school, there isn't room for much else. I haven't been out with a man in nearly a year. As long as Billy is safe and happy, I guess I'm happy, too. If it weren't for your help with the big raise when you made partner, I don't think I could have continued in school without moving back to Dearborn with Mother."

"From what you have said in the past about your relationship with her, that *would have* been a challenge!" Erin concluded.

When the waiter came with their last fill of coffee, Erin asked for the check.

"Erin," Diane said, "before we leave, let me ask one more question, then I'll drop the subject." Do you miss that sheriff of yours?"

Without hesitation Erin answered, "Yes."

* * *

Two months later, Erin was in her office reviewing the deposition for a minor civil trial when Diane knocked lightly, then entered. She was holding a section of the *Detroit Free Press*. "Am I interrupting anything?" she asked.

"No, not at all," Erin answered.

"There is a news item about your sheriff. According to the paper, he has moved up in the world. I circled the article. I'll leave it here on your desk."

As Erin picked up the paper, she looked at the item Diane had mentioned. There was dryness in her throat as she read the brief excerpt from a White House news release:

"Robert Leo Thomas, the junior congressman from Iowa and the newest member of the powerful Agriculture Committee, was singled out and congratulated by President Truman for his heroic war record during a luncheon at the White House."

"Well, Robert, it looks like you really are in a position where you can help those Iowa farmers," Erin whispered softly.

* * *

One afternoon in May, Erin was gazing out her office window. She found herself watching lazy white clouds drift across a brilliant sky. She was thinking about Robert. Erin wondered what he might be doing in Washington. Her thoughts faded when Diane came in with afternoon mail.

"Great news!" a beaming Diane announced. "I received a letter from the University. I've finally graduated from law school!"

"That's wonderful, Diane. I knew a smart woman like you would come through just fine. Looks like I'll be losing a great secretary soon."

"Well, I am taking the bar exam in a few weeks. Then I'm not sure. I don't have any savings, so I guess I'll be staying on with you until I can find a position. I heard at the university's placement office that Wayne County is looking for lawyers," Diane said.

"I'll make some inquires for you at some of the other firms if you like. I'm sure something will turn up. What about a position here? I can talk to Uncle Max."

"No, thanks!" Diane said emphatically.

After Diane left, Erin went through her mail. In the pile was an envelope from the realtor in Spencer. When she opened it, his letter said they were sorry there were not any offers on the property, but school would be out soon and the market should pick up. Placing the letter on her desk, Erin felt sad that Joe had entrusted her with his estate.

* * *

It was June when a glowing Diane walked into Erin's office. "Guess what?" she asked.

"I'll bet you passed the bar exam," Erin answered.

"You got it!" Diane exclaimed. "I'm a real live attorney!"

"I never questioned it for a minute. Why don't you bring Billy to my place this Sunday? If the weather's good we can celebrate with a picnic in the park at Belle Isle!"

"That sounds great. What can I bring?"

"Just you and your son," Erin answered.

* * *

Sunday was a beautiful day. The sun was warm, and the smell of freshly cut grass filled the air. Erin and Diane sat together on a blanket watching seven-year-old Billy scampering about with other children.

"Your boy is getting big," Erin said. "I'm sure you must think a lot about his future."

"Yes, and I worry about the neighborhood where we live. Just as soon as I can afford it, we need to move."

Erin was silent for a time, then asked, "How does a big house on a quiet street with a yard and shade trees sound?"

"Sounds wonderful, but I'm afraid Billy will be grown before I could afford something like that."

"If you're willing, there is a way you can have it now," Erin said.

"And just how would I do that?"

"Joe Butler's office is still unsold and his four bedroom house in Parkston is just waiting for someone to move in."

"I'm not sure I understand," Diane said, frowning.

"What I'm asking is, would you be willing to leave Detroit and move to Parkston, be my partner and help me start a new law practice?"

Diane stared at Erin for a long while. "You mean you plan to leave the firm and move to Iowa?"

"Yes, and I want you and Billy to go with me."

"I don't know what to say," Diane said, overwhelmed by the prospect of Erin's proposal.

"I know it's a big decision. Take a few days and let me know how you feel about all this," she said, sensing her own excitement at what she had proposed.

Erin had thought about the new partnership for some time before mentioning it today. She realized the challenge of starting over, and there was Diane and her son to consider. With no debt on Joe's house or office, plus her substantial savings and the sale of her townhouse, Erin knew they would be fine, even if the practice took a while to grow.

* * *

Erin was in early on Monday, and it surprised her to find Diane was already at her desk.

"I didn't sleep five minutes last night thinking about your offer," Diane said, following Erin into her office.

"Oh, dear Diane, I didn't mean to upset you."

"You didn't upset me. I think it sounds wonderful! The answer is yes!"

"That's great, Diane. Give me an hour, then let's close the door and start making plans for the future!"

After Diane left, Erin lifted the receiver on her telephone and called her uncle's secretary to make an appointment. Erin wanted him to know she would be giving the firm her resignation.

* * *

41

Maxwell Hays was at the breakfast table reading his newspaper on a bright fall morning. He had just put down a glass of orange juice when he noticed an article in the financial section that mentioned the law firm of Hays and Johnson. It stated a small legal firm, located in the town of Parkston, Iowa, had filed a suit against the giant equipment manufacturer, Consolidated Implement Company of Minneapolis. The class action suit named the plaintiff as a Farmers Action Committee, which was asking for a precedent-setting amount of sixteen million dollars for injuries relating to safety issues of CIC's farm equipment division. The article noted the attorney of record, Miss Erin Elizabeth Hays, is the fiancée of the Hon. Robert Leo Thomas, congressional representative from Iowa's seventh district.

Maxwell smiled, put down his paper and began to butter a piece of toast.

THE END

Thanks for reading the story.
I would appreciate any thoughts you might have by
sharing them with me at: rwilley610@comcast.net

Roger Willey